RUNAWAY FIRE

A Novel

DONNA BERTLING

Year of the Book
135 Glen Avenue
Glen Rock, PA 17327

ISBN 10: 1-945670-44-4
ISBN 13: 978-1-945670-44-2

Library of Congress Control Number: 2017954073

Cover images:
Holidays are Kodak Days – Ellis Collection of Kodakiana, David M. Rubenstein Rare Book and Manuscript Library, Duke University.
Firefighters Spraying Water on Buildings and German and Liberty Streets – Courtesy of the Enoch Pratt Free Library, Maryland's State Library Resource Center.

Map image, *Baltimore 1905* – Courtesy of Johns Hopkins Sheridan Libraries

H.L. Menken quotes – reproduced from *The Baltimore Herald* and *Newspaper Days*.

Baltimore, Maryland, 1905
Courtesy of Johns Hopkins Sheridan Libraries

DEDICATION

For Norbert

For Mom and Dad

It was only through a fault and by an error
I heard the cry I ever will remember.
As the fire cast its fatal burning ember
On another fated city of our land.

"Fire, fire," I heard a cry
From every breeze that passes by.
All the world was one sad cry of pity.
Strong men in anguish prayed,
Calling out to the heavens for aid,
While the fire in ruins was laid
Fair Baltimore the beautiful city.

Amid an awful struggle of commotion,
The wind blew a gale from the ocean.
Brave firemen struggled with devotion,
But their efforts all proved in vain.

- Folk Song "Baltimore Fire"

From *Mowry's Songster,* 1905

CHAPTER 1

ANNA

Baltimore
Sunday, February 7, 1904
10:50am

Tight shoelaces strangled my ankles. Step after step, my feet pounding on sidewalk felt like a shoemaker's hammer driving nails into my heels. The pain emancipated me. Propelled me. I couldn't remember ever running this fast, at least not since being a little girl. I reveled in the energy that burned like coal, and encouraged the full flush on my face, the spiral of hair breaking free of my forest green bonnet. I had never felt so vibrant, so free.

How strange.

In recent weeks, I thought I had a hold of myself; I knew what I wanted with full clarity. Now I had no idea why I was running towards a fire, of all places. An urge seemed to drive me closer to harm's way, rather than to the safety of home, sweeping me as fast as a stray page of newspaper caught up in a whirlwind.

With each crossed intersection, I distanced myself from my fiancé, Adrian, and our planned elopement. And pulled away from Papa, our relationship already on soft footing. Intuitively, I knew I would arrive at a destination that would become my hearthstone. What would happen once there was as unknown as tomorrow's headline.

Even stranger, my mother invaded my thoughts. Why? I hadn't seen Mama in seventeen years, and not so much as a vague memory of what she was like had ever stirred the air.

❧

One Year Earlier

The seeds of romance rarely sprout from lack of care. The dry soil of my own heart proved the point. I gave little thought to courtship and marriage, even at the promising age of eighteen, a time when most of my compeers had already packed their wedding gowns in cedar chests and donned the role of lady of the house.

In an effort to see me settled, my father, Dr. Barton Bainbridge, had tried his best to find me a suitable match, which meant someone from his own profession. I had made it clear to all the medical students Papa brought home from the hospital that I had no intention of gracefully carrying out the duties of a doctor's wife. Being the daughter of a physician, I'd had enough of long absences and distracted presences, preferring to live single, fully in the moment. Some would call me a "spinster"... one who does nothing but spin roving. Around and around, an endless cycle, with no goal reached without a man. What a demeaning term, that lacked a male counterpart. I was determined to set my own course forward as "Miss."

But on a warm March morning, with no fanfare, the simple exchange of mail cracked the surface. Though the start was rocky, the suitor packed rich earth. It took root and, with little nurturing, became strong enough to sustain us both.

Ever in a hurry, I rushed out the door and started down the marble steps of the uptown home I shared with Papa. The sound of a popular parlor song swept past my ears like a wayward whisper. A postman, smiling and singing in perfect pitch, delivered the neighborhood's mail.

"*In the good ole summertime, in the good ole sum...*"

"You're blocking my way," I said.

"Are you Miss Anna Bainbridge?"

"Yes. What of it?"

"I have an advertisement for you. Looks real important. Says here it's from the Eastman Kodak Company."

"Give me that, uh, please. Yes, I've been waiting for this."

"I hear a lot of people talking about that new camera. What's it called? The... the..."

"...Brownie. It's called the Brownie."

"That's it. If you don't mind me saying, someone ought to take a picture of you. You're real pretty."

"I must be on my way."

"Certainly, miss. Good day."

A proper "Thank you" hadn't crossed my lips, nor had a polite "Goodbye." Instead, I wondered what might be the matter with the man. I wasn't "real pretty," at least my father had never told me so. Nor had any other man, however few of them had been in my life. Only Elizabeth, my nanny and housekeeper, praised my appearance. Then again, she was the one who coiffed my hair and dressed me and polished my shoes and pinched my cheeks in a futile attempt to bring on a demure blush.

My behavior didn't strike me as rude until I was farther along Saratoga Street and out of sight. I made a half-hearted vow to apologize next time I saw the letter carrier, if ever. Weeks passed, and all was forgotten. By then, I had purchased the Brownie and had been completely taken by it, even to the extent of joining the Brownie Club of America. I devoured every word of the instruction manual that came in the box, all forty-four pages, front to back and yet once more. I learned all about the camera's inner workings, how to load film, snap pictures, and operate the frame-winding key with special care. I had to be cautious, though. Impatience and forgetfulness had already ruined more than one roll of film.

"Please, Papa, please go with me," I begged.

"Anna, you know I have work to do. Maybe another time."

"But the festival is only once a year, and today's the day."

I looked up into Papa's eyes and sought the slightest hint that he might be persuaded. Under heavy lids sat large globes, like black grapes, thickly penetrating yet vacant. A scarred look ringed Papa's eyes, the look of a man who had suffered great hardship from which he had not fully recovered. A seething energy glowed far beyond the scarring, its blue light barely visible, like a fire under a pot on the stove set low for a slow burn.

I often wondered when whatever pained him might be too much, and he'd boil over.

"Please, Papa."

"Well... all right. But only for a little while. You know I don't like to waste my time."

"You won't be wasting time; you'll be with me."

"You know what I mean."

"Yes. Work."

"That's right, Anna. My work is of utmost importance."

While I wanted to know where I fell in my father's list of priorities, I didn't want to sacrifice one second of our day together.

We arrived at Patterson Park just at the peak of activity. Every year, the Children's Playground Association put on a spectacular day of fun for people of all ages. Instead of walking, I bounced along, pulling on Papa's arm to speed his step. I couldn't wait to capture all the festivities on film. Other than Papa, no one was known to me, so I took pictures of strangers eating ice cream, dancing, shooting marbles, boating on the lake, and enjoying the company of their families.

"Papa, why don't you stand over there near the flowers, so I can take your picture?"

"Anna, really, I don't have time for this."

"It will only take a minute."

"Just one more and then we have to go."

I focused on the tall, gaunt form that was my father. But his eyes didn't focus on me. They never seemed to. His gaze peered through me, as if searching for someone better beyond. I wanted to turn around to see who was there.

Clicking the shutter lever, I caught Papa in all his awkwardness. He appeared formal, in total contrast to the flowers nestled around him. The dahlias, daisies and hollyhocks relaxed in more candid poses, some smiling straight up into the sun, others stretching, many dancing in the mild breeze, and a couple facing each other as if lost in the latest gossip.

"Oh, Papa, look... the pagoda. Can we climb to the top? It's such a beautiful day. The view from the observatory must be glorious."

"Maybe next time."

"Maybe next time, maybe next time, always next time," I mumbled.

"What was that, Anna?"

"Nothing, Papa, nothing at all."

"You have enough pictures for now. Let's go home."

Papa turned his back on me, a dismissive move that said there was no sense in pleading. Perhaps he was just avoiding the telltale truth I'd read in his eyes... he was bored with me.

I didn't know why Papa couldn't understand that coming to the park had not only been about taking pictures. It was about sharing my passion for photography and creating our own memories. It was about feeling connected, affirmed.

That's why I had been drawn to photography in the first place. In an instant, the camera united photographer and subject forever. What transpired between them lay bare, out in the open, to be given by one, taken by the other. And the camera never lied. It shed light on the truth in its entire grey scale of good to bad. It showed proof of what happened. It verified existence. I could see that. Why couldn't Papa?

As an only child, I found comfort in photography. When lonesome, I pulled out one or two pictures of made-up siblings and placed them on window seats or the fainting couch for the warmth of company. Sometimes, we just sat by the fire, sipping imaginary tea without needing to speak a word.

I longed for a life worth photographing. Up until then, the reserved world Papa had created shut out the light. So I spied on other worlds through the viewfinder and froze the most engaging moments, then claimed them for my own. I envisioned living inside those pictures, interacting with people as if we knew each other and couldn't live apart for a single moment.

Early on, I learned the historical value of a photograph. My father had encouraged me to read the assortment of national and local newspapers he bought or had compeers in New York send him. He would say, *Knowledge is the key to life itself, Anna. Every decision you make, however small or large, depends on the knowledge you store, and when you choose to unlock it and use it. Don't ever forget that.*

Being younger at the time, I didn't always understand the stories in the newspaper. But the photographs, etchings and engravings certainly caught my eye. They didn't just tell a story; they put me in it, luring Alice to step through the looking glass into a phantasmal universe.

Most memorable was the newspaper "Extra" issued on February 16, 1898, the day after the USS Maine blew up in Havana harbor. Looking for pictures, I found only one when the ship was three weeks old, taken as it had first entered Cuban waters. Later, *The New York Journal* published a picture of the sunken ship's wreckage piercing the water line like Neptune's trident. I wondered who had taken those two divergent shots and what they must be thinking, now that their pictures were all that remained for posterity.

Then, in 1900, Eastman Kodak started mass-producing a box camera that ordinary people could easily use. Through trial and error, I learned all about vertical and horizontal composition, and the need to hold the camera steady and press gently on the shutter lever to capture a clear shot. The experience taught me to view life from different angles, up and down and side to side, and to be steady and sure of my own decisions before pressing onward.

This box camera, with its tiny aperture, opened my eyes. It let the light in. I wanted Papa's world to blossom, too. If only he would have come out of the shadows into full sunshine, our lives would not have been so unnaturally black and white.

"Good night, Anna."

"Oh, Papa, I can't wait to get the pictures developed."

"Good night, Anna."

"Don't you want to see them, too, especially the ones of you?"

"Good night, Anna."

"I'll put them in a new book, maybe a pink one. Wouldn't that be lovely, Papa? Papa? Well, good night, Papa."

Our weekend over, my father retreated to his study, and I to my bedroom, where the hope of sweet memories of the day faded like a photograph left too long in the sun.

CHAPTER 2

ADRIAN

In the early 1900s, Gibson Girls were all the rage. They were coquettish and fun though fey, burying their heads in the latest edition of *Harper's Bazaar* or *Vogue*. They copied what they saw, powdering and rouging, masking the countenance within. Atop their heads, chignons were piled so high and round they looked like funnel clouds. These women swept men off their feet. Sometimes, even me, I don't mind admitting.

I loved the ladies and, at twenty-four, had wooed more than a few. I liked going out, having fun. Attractive as the Gibson Girls were, many lacked substance beneath the skin. As soon as courtship got serious, they plied me with nosy questions.

"Adrian, what do you really want to do with your life beyond delivering the mail?"

"How much money does a letter carrier earn?"

"Why don't you buy an automobile? We could visit more places."

"Do you have a telephone?"

"A phonograph player?"

How could they be blamed? The world was changing as fast as the calendar. Factories popped up everywhere, offering jobs, and manufactured clothing and merchandise to consumers. Workers in New York laid track for an underground train system, while the Wright Brothers set their sights much higher. Oil gushed in Texas, boosting the emerging auto industry. Dress designers shortened hemlines to the ankle, making it easier for ladies to step in and out of vehicles gracefully, or ride bicycles without getting long petticoats caught in the spokes. Americans were struck with—what did the newspapers call it?—Wanderlust. People dared to imagine that one day they might be able to travel under the earth, in the air, or seated comfortably in their own automobiles. They found something new almost every time they shopped. Sewing machines, ping-pong tables, vacuum cleaners, even teabags and chocolate bars. These products excited women, made their lives easier, more enjoyable, and elicited envy from friends and families. Ladies' dreams of leisure erased their everyday drudgery.

My meager wallet could never compete with the fat bank accounts that attracted these women. Besides, I loved being a postman and had no aspirations beyond that. I didn't mind walking at all and enjoyed riding the trolley. What need was there for a Ford Runabout or a Curved Dash Oldsmobile? And a telephone was far too impersonal; I preferred talking to people face to face. As for a phonograph player, it would just get in the way. I enjoyed making my own music. The type of woman whose love came with such costly conditions was not the type I wanted for a wife.

Without a doubt, Anna could not be mistaken for a Gibson Girl. She embodied the antithesis of style and affectation. Her skin, as pale as cake flour, showed no trace of artificial color. Her eyes didn't flirt; they glossed a thick caramel. Her features read nondescript, her countenance neither beautiful nor unpleasant.

But I liked Anna just the way she was. The daring hint of leg she showed when skipping down the marble steps from the stoop to the street. Her bubbly walk, so full of sarsaparilla. She always seemed to be in such a hurry that her short legs would fall into a syncopated rhythm, as if dancing to a Ragtime tune. And those long, soft chestnut curls. They just couldn't be contained by any hairpin or bonnet. At least one shiny tendril always ran astray from her chignon, its impropriety oblivious to the wearer. She wore muted or dark clothing, nothing that stood out or made her look as if she were trying to impress. Just the same, she caught my eye.

I met Anna quite by accident, or so it seemed. I had set my cap for the young lady of the large townhouse on the west side as I delivered the post in her neighborhood, and waited patiently to make myself known. I made sure our meeting would happen on purpose, although casually, so my motives wouldn't be revealed too soon. Crossing the street, I headed towards Anna's home and broke into a little parlor song chosen just for her.

In the good ole summertime...

Anna didn't seem to care. Instead, she tried to push past me. I was not about to give up so easily. To soften her mood, I handed her an Eastman Kodak Company advertisement along with a gentle compliment.

...someone ought to take a picture of you... you're real pretty.

That didn't do the trick either.

Anna took off without saying goodbye. All I saw was the bow on the back of her dress, swaying to and fro like a metronome in 4/4 time. Her behavior wasn't off-putting in the least. Just the opposite. It made me smile. In Anna I saw qualities I looked for in a wife. She was as spirited and determined as snowdrops, the first flower to break through the earth's cold crust each year, bold enough to rush the spring.

Let the other guys have the Gibson Girls, I thought.

Anna was the one for me but she had vanished into the uptown hustle-bustle. I wasn't ready to surrender the torch I carried for her, though. Experience had taught me that the virtue of patience took little investment and almost always paid a return. I planned to wait and search for another opportunity to become more appealing to Anna.

"Hold on there," I said, chuckling.

Anna was so excited that she had started to step off the trolley before it came to a complete stop. I grabbed her by the hand and slipped my other arm around her slim waist.

For once, Anna was not attached to her Brownie. I had asked her to leave it home this time, in part to protect the camera from harm, but more so out of selfishness; I wanted to have Anna all to myself.

"Oh, Adrian, you deceived me. This is bigger and more beautiful than you described. Look at that grand entrance, all those twinkling lights. They're everywhere. Why, it's as bright as day."

"I wanted you to be surprised."

"Electric Park. I had no idea there was such a place."

"Well then, what are we waiting for?"

"And to think the trolley line ends right here."

"That's what it's supposed to do. This is a trolley park."

"What does that mean?"

"The trolley company helped build this place. Entrance is free to the public, but it's so remote, people have to pay the trolley to get here. And that's how the company makes its money."

"What a clever idea."

Electric Park was an amusement and horseracing venue taking up twenty-four acres northwest of the city, quite a distance from downtown. It offered a wide variety of entertainment activities and was one of my favorite places to take a lady friend.

"They're showing a short, silent film called *Life of An American Fireman*. Would you like to see it?"

"Yes, I would. I've never seen a movie," she answered.

"What? Never?

"No. Wait a minute, Adrian. What's that?" She pointed to a large raised disc mounted to a floor as clean as spit-shine.

"Oh, you mean the Human Roulette Wheel?"

"Yes, I want to try that first."

"Anna, it's not a very ladylike thing to do."

"Why?"

"Well, you'd have to sit on that giant circle. When the music starts, you get spun around. There it goes now. See, it's going faster and faster, and one by one, everybody flies off."

"Oh, let's get in line for the next round. That looks like a grand time."

"Well, if you really want to. But you'll have to hold on to your skirt, so your, ah, pardon the expression, bloomers don't show."

"I don't care if they do."

Anna surprised me with such brazen disregard for propriety, but I didn't think less of her. Anna's free-wheeling spirit made me love her even more. She insisted on sitting at the very center, so our ride would be the longest. Whizzing in circles, we saw the park lights swirl around us like spun sugar coating a paper cone.

"Whew, I'm dizzy," Anna said, when she stood up.

The broadness of her smile told me that Anna didn't mind one bit. She was having the time of her life. We rode the carousel and both roller coasters, then laughed ourselves giddy on the Shoot-The-Chutes. I protected Anna in the boat and took the brunt of the spray when we hit the water at the bottom of the chute. Anna wanted to turn around and get right back on the ride, even though I was soaked.

"Save something for next time," I said.

"I don't want to. I want to experience it all now."

Anna seemed so happy that I couldn't deny her any of the park's attractions. We enjoyed the vaudeville acts and music by the popular park band, led by Signor Vincent Del Manto. When the ensemble played *The Electric Park March*, we clapped our hands and stomped our feet along with the crowd. Once I really got to know Anna, I discovered this was the first time in her life she had felt in step with others, part of a community. What a wonderful feeling for her, and a great honor for me. I was so glad to be responsible for her happiness, something I never felt in the company of Gibson Girls.

Finally, we took in the movie. Anna was enthralled. She said I had saved the best for last. "Moving pictures. Can you imagine that? Thousands of photographs coming to life. I would love to know how they made that happen. Thank you, Adrian, for such a wonderful night."

"It was my pleasure."

As we rode the trolley home, Anna fell into a pensive mood. I felt concerned for her.

"Are you tired? Was it all too much for you, Anna?"

"No, it was perfect. I was just thinking. Adrian... it's time we told Papa about us. Elizabeth already suspects I'm seeing someone. She questioned why I was going out alone at dusk tonight. I told her not to worry but I know she's confused. It's unlike me to be so vague. I would never lie to her."

"I'm not sure now is..."

"Oh, Adrian, he's going to love you just as much as I do. Please come to dinner. Shall we say Friday night?"

Anna had told me about her father's stern nature, so I was hesitant. I arrived on time nonetheless, bearing a simple corsage of three pink carnations gathered with a mint green ribbon. Elizabeth took the flowers and my hat, and escorted me into the kitchen, where a small table had been set. I thought it odd that we were going to sup there, while the large, accommodating dining room sat empty. I brightened when Anna, wearing my corsage, came into the room on the arm of her father.

Anna had assured me that Dr. Bainbridge and I would be drawn to one another but it didn't happen. We repelled. I can still hear the doctor's deliberate, drawn-out baritone filling the room.

"A letter carrier?"

"Yes, sir. I deliver the post in your neighborhood."

"So you can read, at least?"

"Papa, don't..." Anna chimed in.

"Doctor Bainbridge, I do not have degrees in science or medicine, but I do know how an invited guest should be treated."

"You were invited to dinner. Dinner is now over. Please leave."

"Papa, no."

Anna started to cry. I was surprised to see her father remain blithe in light of her pain, more determined in his ways.

"I do not approve, Anna. I will not pretend otherwise."

"Listen to me, Papa. Adrian, please don't go."

Taking my straw hat from Elizabeth in the foyer, I heard words of derision spill from the kitchen and emphasis on one, final say-so.

"Anna, that man is nothing but a *prole*."

"Papa, how dare you refer to Adrian as lowly and unimportant. He means everything to me."

"Everything? Anna, you have encouraged this man without my knowledge. You have seen him without a chaperone. You have deceived me."

"Papa, no. If you could only see him the way I do, you wouldn't be so resistant."

Anna began to sob; the doctor became more impassive. What an indigestible exchange. I couldn't stomach it.

"Stop this insolence at once. I am your father."

Anna ran through the foyer and up the stairs to her room.

"Anna..." I called, wanting so desperately to comfort her.

I went home in a fretful state that night, thinking this was the end of our love affair. I would never see my darling Anna again. With one single, slashing word... *prole*... Dr. Bainbridge had cut me out of his daughter's life with all the deftness of a surgeon's incision.

Chapter 3

ANNA

Sunday, February 7, 1904
10:23 am

Every Sunday morning, Baltimore city firefighters donned their dress uniforms for inspection. On Sunday, February 7, 1904, the men of Engine Co. 15 had no time to change back into firefighting gear. At 10:23am, a trouble signal sounded at their station near the Bromo Seltzer tower, coming from the automatic alarm on Box 854. The problem arose from the John E. Hurst building near Baltimore and Liberty Streets. A combination engine was sent with a crew to conduct a quick survey and, after seeing no trouble, the firemen returned to the station house satisfied. Being the weekend, there wasn't an overnight watchman on duty to allow them access into the building.

Sometimes, in its early stages, a fire disguises itself. It waits in hiding, under boxes, in the corner, down an elevator shaft, out of sight or smell of the most seasoned firefighters. Once the coast clears, the villain sheds its mask, revealing a disfigured determination to destroy all that is held most dear.

No one knows definitively how The Great Baltimore Fire of 1904 started. Some think an errant cigarette fell through a broken deadeye in a sidewalk window the night before. The sparks slunk overnight, then flared while most of Baltimore was eating breakfast or getting dressed for church, as was I.

Inching towards the bedroom mirror, my image grew from child to woman. In my underclothes, I observed the natural taking-in and letting-out of my body. The girl I once knew had developed into a woman who, until this moment, had escaped my attention. Now that my heart swelled to the fullness of one in love, the tailoring could be appreciated. I vowed that when I got dressed and left this room, knowing it might be for the last time, any remnants of the girl would be left behind.

I stared at my reflection while fastening every hook and buttoning every loop of my Sunday best... a black, bell-shaped dress, topped with a cinched waistcoat in deep green velvet. Black braiding, as knotty as my stomach, piped the jacket. The veil of the matching hat framed my face staidly, the bonnet itself sitting in want for the more ornate, youthful style of the day, which I found too fussy. A simple spray of iridescent feathers curled out of the hatband, while the brim rose higher on one side than the other, giving the impression that I, myself, was off-kilter.

I did feel out of sorts because I planned to act on the first independent decision of my nineteen years. I was going to elope... and in doing so, violate the strict standards of my father, the "esteemed Dr. Bainbridge," as he was called so often, it seemed a royal title.

Papa's field was cardiology. With his many prestigious medical degrees came the assumption that he was an authority on all matters of the heart. I begged to differ.

For a split second, I thought I caught sight of Papa in the mirror, just over my shoulder. He needn't have been there. His words alone would shadow me, as they always did.

Anna, only I know what is in your best interest.

I lowered my head shamefaced, knowing how hurt Papa would be when he found out his only child had married behind his back and against his wishes.

Despite the obvious deception, I loved my father dearly.

Even though Papa must have loved me, too, difficult as it was to tell, any show of it had always been on his terms. He rarely gave of himself fully. His body would be present, his attention... distant. Fatherly affection never exceeded a feathery kiss on the forehead, barely discernible. I craved so much more.

This morning, his full attention focused on the hospital and medical student working hand in hand with him. As I donned my leather gloves, I pictured the two of them as they examined patients and updated charts. My father and the student would hit it off just fine, talking about aortas and ventricles, blood flow and blockage. But change the subject to the bloodlines that connect father to daughter, and Papa would have a hard time finding a pulse. Someone outside his circle might perceive his long days at the hospital as nothing more than the demands of his job and his dedication to heal and teach others to find cures. Elizabeth probably thought he wanted to be away from a home devoid of his wife. I knew better.

The reason for Papa's long absences loomed like the canopy over my bed, where Papa had never tucked me in with a fairytale or fable. I knew as long as he was absorbed in his work, he was absolved of his fatherly duties. He didn't want to be bothered with everyday cares of raising a child. To him, a diseased body was much easier to keep alive than the emotional ties that bind one to another. It demanded less commitment; it proved to be less painful. And wasn't it the sworn duty of a doctor to ease pain? Even his own?

I reached into the chifforobe and lifted a small stack of photographs to pack in my bag—pictures sacred to me, because they had been taken on one of those rare father-daughter outings. I thumbed through each one in the order the day had unfolded as we strolled around the commons of Baltimore's Washington Monument. Most of the pictures caught him lecturing as if I were one of his medical students. Papa did most of the talking; I just listened. It wasn't fun, but what he said was meant only for my ears. I tried to attribute sweetness and thoughtfulness to his words that didn't exist. I was really reshaping his speeches, forcing the sentences into an ill-fitting substitute for the cozy bedtime stories I always wanted and never got.

At all times, conduct yourself as a lady, Anna. There is no greater tribute to your fair gender.

I sat down on the bed and laughed at the remembrance. That bit of advice had not found a place in my life, and its vacancy often landed me in hot water. Whenever my conscience weighed propriety against honesty, the latter tipped the scales. I found small talk and politeness to be forms of trickery. Tactfulness masked the truth. I had no interest in communicating with people who elevated circumspection to virtue. Sometimes honesty hurt; it inflicted pain. I thought it was worth it, every word.

Anna, you are never to see that man again.

—He has a name and not the one you called him.

I don't care to repeat it. He means nothing to me.

—But he means something to me, Papa. I want to marry him.

You will not.

—Yes, I will. I have come of age. I can make my own decisions.

I am your father, and you will marry the man I choose. Why are you being so intractable?

—I learned it from you.

Elizabeth, is this how you have raised my daughter to speak to me? Is this what I pay you handsomely for?

—Not at all, sir. I'm terribly sorry.

I berated myself once more. I was failing to live up to my own beliefs. I should have been forthright with Papa about the wedding. Deceiving him was not my intention. It was just that I had no idea how he would react to such rebellion and disrespect. What would he do?

Most times, my father's expressions of love, anger, joy and pain took a dilatory route. Our arguments, in particular, were often emotionally one-sided. I would be reduced to tears, while Papa stayed reserved, even removed.

He was such a quiet man. It was his body language that spoke for him in the subtlest of ways. If I reached up to take his arm, he'd often find reasons to escape my grasp. He'd straighten his tie, search his pocket for a handkerchief, or circle the wedding band he still wore around his ring finger, seventeen years after losing Mama.

The ring adorned my father's perfect hands, smooth and delicate and well groomed, as if they had been gloved since birth, protected from life's rough surfaces. The look of them made Papa appear open and friendly, a deceit I knew all too well.

Only through our "important talks" did I feel that Papa showed fatherly interest in me. Even though most were aimed well above my head, I could recount them verbatim. Every word still hangs in my memory like crisp, white sheets lined up to dry, each inscribed with poetry or aphorisms, flapping in the breeze, waiting for the mature moment when I would know when to take one down and wrap myself in it.

Remember who you are, and how important I am, and all that I can do for you. I want you to pay attention, Anna, and learn.

No, I was not going against Papa out of spite or rejection, but out of love. For Adrian. He had taught me the definition of unconditional love, no strings attached, no scars or distant light. His heart received me as I was, as if Adrian detected something in me, a unique quality about to blossom in deep, rich layers.

Adrian's hands bore paper cuts and the leathered wear and tear of a man who worked outdoors. His eyes revealed a gentle soul. Under a mantel of brown hair, they sparkled blue and welcomed me like a hearth stoked to a warm glow. I couldn't wait to pull up a chair and stare into their infinite depth forever.

Picking up my Brownie and a small suitcase, I caught my reflection one last time before leaving. I said goodbye to my childhood, my bedroom, and the only home I had ever known. I hoped I wouldn't run into Elizabeth on the way out because I didn't want to have to weigh truth against lie concerning what I was up to and with whom. I prayed that Elizabeth was sleeping in, as she often did on Sundays, and would attend church later. That way, our paths wouldn't cross. Once married, I would explain to my dear nanny why I hadn't confided in her and how much I yearned for her blessing and support.

Grabbing a bag of biscuits with apricot jam I had packed earlier and left on the bench in the hallway, I opened the front door. The stuffiness inside my home cowered in the face of the cold February air. I was undaunted.

I stepped across the threshold and onto the marble stoop. To my surprise, a gust of wind raced down the street and spun me like a scolding parent, trying to force me back inside. Its fearsome howl sounded a warning not to do what I was about to do. I refused to obey; nothing would stop me.

With one hand, I clenched my things and pressed my hat against my head. With the other, I grabbed the round brass doorknob and tried to pull the carved mahogany door closed. The wind flexed its muscle; it became more heavy-handed, more pleading. I denied it with a vengeance. I pulled harder, with all my might, only easing up when I heard the click of the lock, a small sound that intoned so much finality.

With one single catch, I closed off my past. I turned and faced the future which, in that instant, broadened as boundless as the outdoors.

Momentarily, I gave in to the wind, using it for my own gain. I drew in a deep, powerful breath, and descended the first step. The experience made me lightheaded. I was easing onto a high wire, balancing above my old life on one side and a new one on the other. To prove my resolution, I skipped down the remaining steps, onto the sidewalk and down the street.

As I headed several blocks east, I placed as much distance as possible between my intentions and the temptation to take one last look back. Even though I walked with all the confidence a five-foot frame could project, that same swirl of doubt continued to nip at my heels. The shadow of my father's slow and steady voice trailed not far behind.

End this romance now.

I walked faster. I had agreed to meet Adrian at St. Alphonsus Church, where we would exchange vows in the rectory after the early Mass, and time was running late.

My father would lose track of the hour, too, at the hospital and, as usual, end up staying there well into the evening. He wouldn't find out about the wedding until it was beyond stopping. He couldn't prevent the nuptials anyway. I was an adult by law.

I paused to switch my suitcase from my left hand to the right. I had purchased the bag myself, having never needed one before. Many girls of my age and breeding had long ago been packed off to boarding school. Not me. My education took place close to home. It seemed that Papa wanted me near, even though he kept me at arm's length. And any hopes of a vacation away had always melted into illusion.

What did that say about a person who supposedly had everything? That I lived a life so contained and chained down that it had no movement, no flow, and the only escape was to steal away with a single suitcase that held next to nothing?

I had packed only a few of my favorite clothes and shoes, toiletries, and the bag of biscuits with apricot jam to share with Adrian on the trolley ride to his apartment, soon to be my own home. And, of course, I carried my Brownie box camera, the same one Adrian had mentioned to me several months earlier. I rarely left home without it. Inside a small satin drawstring purse, I had placed ten rolls of unexposed film that held six frames each. Before leaving the house, I slipped the reticule inside the deep fan pocket of my dress. My fan was left behind. Film had become too precious a commodity to risk losing and my pocket served as the safest hiding place.

As a measure of assurance, I pressed my hand against the pouch in my dress. I didn't sense danger, didn't smell smoke starting to swirl in the wailing wind.

When I reached the church, Monsignor Vilkas stood at the door, greeting worshipers as they entered the vestibule.

"Good morning, Monsignor."

"Well, here comes the bride," he chuckled. "Come in, come in. Get out of this dreadful weather, my dear. You're so tiny, you'll blow like a maple leaf all the way to Charles Street before anyone can catch you. Now let me see. You can stow your things over here."

As we walked towards an empty confessional, the priest stared at me, at first with amusement, then apprehension.

"Are you all right, Anna?"

"Yes, of course, Monsignor. Why do you ask?"

"I've known you your whole life, my dear. I baptized you. And through all of our pre-nuptial meetings with your intended, I had no doubt that you were doing the right thing, even knowing how much your father would disapprove. But now I'm not so sure. Are you getting cold feet?"

I couldn't imagine what Monsignor Vilkas meant. For a second, I wondered if he had spotted a sliver of uncertainty, something as thin and mysterious as a communion wafer.

Before I could respond, my attention was drawn to the volume of voices growing outside, far from normal Sunday salutations. Without parting words, I left the monsignor's company and ran for the door. There, a small crowd of people looked up, their eyes riveted to the sky and the buildings that reached for it. Within seconds, we all heard unmistakable cries coming from just a few blocks away, cries every citizen feared to the core.

"Fire!"

"Fire!"

"Call for the fire brigade!"

Chapter 4

ADRIAN

Sunday, 10:20am

"Good morning, Adrian," the trolley driver said.

"It is a good morning, Robert. The best possible."

"You're looking right spiffy. What's the occasion?"

"Something really special."

"Is this the beginning of another one of your riddles?"

"No, I'll tell you all about it next week, when I return to work."

"The trolley won't be the same without you serenading us to and fro."

"Fine with me. I'll be serenading someone else."

"I see," the driver said, a slight smile on his face.

I shivered as the pantograph sizzled across the line from the eastern outskirts of Baltimore to downtown. Head to toe, I was decked out in my best bib and tucker. It wasn't enough. The cold penetrated my light dress coat and my trilby warmed my head but not my ears. I longed for my layered work uniform on such a blustery day. Far from dapper, it provided more comfort. I could always count on that three-piece uniform with its long, thick overcoat to keep me as toasty as the hot brick placed at the bottom of my lonesome bed.

Crowded benches might have generated warmth. But the streetcar was nearly empty, so all I could do was hug my arms against the chill.

I thumbed through a mental checklist of all that I had done to transform my simple apartment into a home for Anna. What I had to offer would be no match for... what are they called? ...tapestry *fauteuils*, and crystal beaded chandeliers and Art Nouveau wallpaper adorning the Bainbridge home. Those things

23

didn't inspire Anna; they left her cold, even ill at ease. My place lacked all that fanciness. I had furnished it with laughter and appointed it with love, more to Anna's sense of style.

When I took her to see my home, I knew it was the first time she had been alone with a man in his apartment. I stood back as she looked around, so she wouldn't feel threatened. And I let her tour the bedroom and bathroom on her own.

"This is really, umm, intimate," Anna said, meaning cozy, I guess, maybe a little too cozy. Perhaps, she was searching for some private space to call her own. Putting on a confident face, she said, *"I know I'll be happy here, anywhere you are."* Somehow, I wasn't assured.

For our wedding night, I wanted to make everything extra special. My plain wood floors had been swept and scrubbed. New bed linens... cream-colored sheets and a pale pink chenille cover with burgundy rosettes... had been chosen with Anna in mind, then pressed and tucked into place just so. Though sparsely stocked, the kitchen sparkled. The firebox in the coal stove sat poised for the strike of a match. On the small end table by the window in the living room rested a demure arrangement of snowdrops to greet Anna when I unlocked the door. Their sweet smell would precede the sight of their pure white blossoms. As for the bathroom, well, matters of the bathroom I was too much of a gentleman to think about. That would be Anna's domain.

A small chocolate cake beckoned from the kitchen table, where I had set two plates, two forks, and two cloth napkins. Two of this and two of that. Two of everything from now on. Just setting the table for two had made me smile and weep at the same time. Two emotional responses.

It didn't matter that I had spent almost all of my savings to make this tiny four-room flat the best it could be for Anna. It's what I had saved my money for... a bride, a wife, a mother to the many children I hoped would be blessed upon the two of us becoming one.

I was used to being alone most of my life. I was the only child of Margaret and Angus Crosby, a hard-working couple who spent every last dollar they earned to sail steerage to the United States from Scotland long before I came along. Hailing from a poor village in the Central Lowlands, they had hung their dreams on the belief that America must be paved in gold. Unfortunately, when they arrived in Baltimore, they found nothing so gleaming, not even the glint of a lost copper penny. Becoming citizens had turned out to be far more difficult than anticipated. With no American sponsor to guide them, they had to find their own way and work seven days a week just to break even. They could afford precious little time for joy or me.

Rin alang noo, son. Mrs. Williams is waitin' fur ye (or Mrs. Warren or Mrs. Hook, or whomever my parents entrusted with my care).

No matter who looked out for my welfare, sitters or teachers, they found me an intelligent and absorbent student. I loved reading, especially books on science and history. I was often left with neighbors, while my parents tried to grow their milk and cheese delivery business. I made friends easily, but yearned to belong to a large, close-knit family. Maybe that's why I eventually became a letter carrier.

On my route, I got a chance to peek into other people's lives and live my own dreams vicariously. I discovered that so many families came in fours, fives, even tens, with grandparents, aunts and uncles, and cousins. Here, a flyer from Sears & Roebuck to the Wood family. There, a party invitation for all six of the Hogans, or a letter for Mr. Hensley from his brother in England. Every day, preparing for the route, I wondered what I'd slip in the mail slot that would bring people closer and make them happy. My job made me feel good, worth something, in a way no other could have. But my own mailbox often sat empty.

Over time, eavesdropping proved to be a poor surrogate for real relationships. I dreamed of having a family life of my own, surprising my daughters with pretty new dresses. And giving and going to parties. I wanted a wife who shared those same dreams.

Oh, I knew I could charm the ladies. Even if they weren't happy with my bank account, they loved my corny jokes.

A little boy was tending a garden. A lady walked by and said, "Are those flowers poppies?" Without hesitation, the child looked up and replied, "No, they're mommy's."

And they liked to hear me sing popular tunes without need of sheet music or accompaniment. I favored a silly song from 1903. *If money talks/it ain't on speaking terms with me.*

Would my jokes and songs be enough to keep Anna happy for a lifetime? That thought occupied my mind constantly.

"Next stop, the Main Post Office."

The conductor's sudden call pierced my cold ears. I stood and stepped off the trolley.

"See you in a few days, Robert."

"A happier man, I imagine."

I should have stayed onboard for several more blocks. But there was time to walk off nervous energy. And I had plenty of it. After all, I was about to take the biggest step of my life.

And it gave me the opportunity to savor the beauty of the Main Post Office building, where I picked up my deliveries before going out on rounds. It brought me pleasure each morning, so it seemed only fitting to include this happy ritual on my wedding day.

Most of my co-workers saw the building as just a place to earn a wage. Not me. I liked to gaze at its ornate Italian architecture, its double-pitched roof with nine regal towers. I used to count each one before starting my day, in the belief that it might well have been possible for someone to make off with one overnight. I stared at the dozens of large-paned windows that reflected the skyline as if mirroring a perfect world. The building's grandeur always seemed to rub off on my demeanor and elicit a smile as I entered the door under the banner of Old Glory.

The importance of delivering the mail was never lost on me. I connected "How is everyone there?" to "We are all fine here." I loved my job; it allowed me to meet so many different people.

Good morning, Miss Michalski. How was your trip to Paris and London?

Nice day, isn't it Mrs. Dorsey? Did you finish that oil portrait of your son, Christopher, and his wife? I'd love to see it.

Here's your mail, Mrs. Woodward. How's the mister? And your mother, Mary Lynn?

I would sing and whistle and hum along uptown sidewalks and inside tenement stairwells farther east. And walking from door to door each day kept my physique lean. It meant I could eat seconds at the table when affordable, which wasn't often. Oh my, did I enjoy a good meal—biscuits and jam being my favorite, and roast chicken with buttered noodles, and apple pie with a slice of cheddar.

As I strolled the familiar streets leading to church, I had to adjust my felt derby against the wind more than once. I lifted my lapels and put my hand in my pocket to finger the time-worn bands my bride and I would soon wear "until death do us part." They had been my parents' wedding rings. Sad to say, I had slipped them off their fingers myself after they died together in an accident. While making their deliveries in a rickety cart, something spooked their horse. Old "Bucket" took off like a bangtail and couldn't negotiate a sharp turn.

I held no superstition in using my parents' wedding rings. They represented a love that even death couldn't part. I promised Anna the same, and she sealed it with a kiss. Funny how promises are broken and beliefs shatter into pieces too small for the dustpan.

Only a block or two away, I heard the voice of a coworker, who lived nearby.

"Adrian, look up. Smoke."

"Where do you think it's coming from, Sam?"

"Well, I'd say seven or eight blocks due west."

"What?"

If true, that was dangerously close to St. Alphonsus and Anna's home.

My imagination started to run wild. I thought maybe a candle had gotten knocked over during Mass and set fire to the altar linens. Or reckless sparks had escaped an unattended fireplace, perhaps in Anna's neighborhood or, worse yet, in her home. I couldn't lose Anna so close to claiming her for my wife.

I took flight.

"Adrian, wait. What's the matter?" Sam yelled.

I ignored him and moved even faster, dodging a stack of newspapers sitting next to a vendor's stand. I knocked into a man coming around a corner and kept going without apology. As I crossed Calvert Street, my brand-new patent leather boots splashed water in a puddle by the curb. My socks and the cuffed hem of my dress pants became soaked. I didn't care.

Sam, of course, couldn't have understood my reaction to the fire. We didn't know each other that well. Our morning work routine consisted of challenging each other with jokes and riddles as we stuffed our mailbags. Nothing more. Concern and perhaps curiosity must have pushed him to follow me at a safe distance.

The closer I got, the more frightened I became. I sensed an undercurrent, a portent that wouldn't play out well. There was so much commotion converging at once. Clanging bells assaulted the Sunday morning calm, and a fire engine almost ran me down.

"Get out of the way. Get back," a police officer yelled. You... get back on the sidewalk."

"I have to get to the fire."

I kept running anyway. My eyes stayed focused on the sky. I didn't see the patch of ice on the sidewalk hidden in the penumbra of a five-story building. I fell hard. My hat went flying and a tear in my pants near the right knee revealed a bleeding gash. Passersby rushed to my side and helped me to my feet. I stood shaken and in pain. The police officer handed me my hat and asked about my well-being.

"You should tend to that wound right away," he said.

I looked down at the cut and felt blood trickle into my sock garters. Attempting to walk became impossible. I pulled a handkerchief from my pocket and pressed it to my wound, all the while wondering where my sweet bride might be.

As the small crowd of people who had helped me dispersed, I leaned against a pole and reached into my pocket to make sure the rings had not escaped during the fall. My relief in finding them there was short-lived. Soon the undercurrent swelled into panic and pained me more than my injury. I didn't know what to make of it. I wasn't normally a worrier or a negative thinker.

I couldn't give way to anything as impractical as fear. My leg ached and bled too badly. It no longer supported me. Having no choice, I lowered myself, sat down on the thin, cold curb, and tried my best to recover.

CHAPTER 5

ANNA

Sunday, 10:48am

Run, run, run, the clamant wind cried. I obeyed without question. I had left my suitcase and the bag of biscuits behind at church and carried only my camera, already loaded with film. Still tucked in my fan pocket were rolls of unexposed film and a mechanical pencil taken from my father's office to identify the frames.

As a wedding gift, I had planned to present my groom with a photograph album of honeymoon pictures and wanted to include descriptions of where we were and what we were doing.

All of that would have to be put on hold for the time being. Something more important caught my attention right then and there, and it wouldn't wait, not even for Adrian.

Crossing Saratoga cattycorner, I ran towards Liberty and Baltimore Streets. I had no idea what to expect once there. When I rounded the milliner's shop at the end of the block, my feet stopped so abruptly that my body kept moving and tipped forward. My breathing became heavy with an incongruous mixture of fear and wonderment. My eyes widened and fixed on an impending disaster.

Black smoke streamed out of every seam in the fourth floor of the John Hurst & Company dry goods store. A worse place for a fire could not have been picked by the devil himself. The warehouse had just been stocked with merchandise floor to ceiling. For protection against breakage, many boxes had been packed with excelsior—combustible ringlets of wood. The crates sat ready for store buyers from the southland to visit Baltimore and make their purchases after the winter thaw, then return to their home states to sell for profit. These serried goods towered like bonfire tinder.

Firefighters had to act fast. But, due to the weight they pulled, fire horses could only gallop about eight blocks without stopping to rest. Luckily, a fire company was close by.

The thunder of hooves hitting cobblestones roared down the street and intensified until a team of three fire horses, massive beasts, each weighing a ton, stormed in my direction from Engine Co. 15, led by Captain John Kahl. They pulled a water tower that could stretch to the higher floors. Narrow streets challenged the driver maneuvering into position. Firefighters jumped off while the horses were still in motion. They made quick work of unlocking the spring release to raise the laddered tower. A steamer fire engine followed, carrying hostler, Mark Hill, and another firefighter, who used the piston-driven boiler to drive the water in the hose at full pressure up the tower.

The street measured only thirty-five feet wide, making the firefighting equipment crowd the area like another building. Everyone, including me, was hemmed in.

My eyes darted from one fireman to the next as they hooked up hoses and grabbed axes, getting ready to barge into the building. The hostler started unhitching the horses from the vehicle to move them away from potential harm and cover them in blankets to ward off the cold.

I had never seen such a spectacle before. Smoke gushing, people screaming, firemen surging, hooves clomping. Alarming as it was, the dark beauty of danger drew me closer.

This experience was foreign to anything I had ever known. Mine had been a life protected these nineteen years, sheltered from trials and trouble. What was I doing in the midst of an unfolding tragedy?

I felt the sensation of stepping into a photograph of someone else and being held captive in its frame. At the same time, I knew I belonged there. Against all better judgment and previous experience... and any of my father's advice flapping in the breeze... I decided to stay put.

An instinct flared up inside me like the striking of a match. It burned with the resonant smell of duty, an urge to step forward

and, in some way, participate. Even though this sensati(
new to me, it fit like the fabled glass slipper.

Obviously, I wasn't dressed to do what was necessary. Without giving it a thought, I stripped the black leather gloves off my hands and tossed them in the gutter. I lifted the dotted Swiss veil that covered my face and pushed it up over the brim of my hat. I backed up as far as I could across the street and stood against a brick wall. Planting my feet, I steadied the camera against my torso, tucked my elbows tight to my sides, composed the shot, held my breath, and pressed the shutter.

As white light refracted in aperture, a rush of adrenaline surged through my body. It charged me with extraordinary energy, an ability to stop time, capture life in my hand. In a split second, I morphed into a godlike force that made the camera work miracles. I shamelessly exalted in my power.

I fixed on Captain Kahl and his firemen as they pushed through the glass door of the dry goods store. While they searched for fire inside... *Boom!*

An explosion shattered the Sunday morning reverence. The roof and upper floors of the Hurst building blew off with such surprise and bass-tone force that my bones vibrated in rhythm and my heart quivered like a tuning fork. The reverberation of the explosion raged for blocks, rapping on windows, thrumming on doors, racing away from me until it was finally consumed by the pitch and howl of the wind.

I looked up, shocked to see that I had been blown to the ground. Others who had lost their footing slowly crept to their knees, checking for injuries. No one seemed to be hurt, save the concussive ringing in our ears.

I picked up my camera, relieved to find it undamaged. Gingerly getting up myself, I brushed away small pieces of gravel embedded in my palm, and slapped at the fine layer of dust that clung to my dress like a lace wedding veil.

Burning debris rained down, catching a second building and an electrical pole on fire. Storefront awnings caught next, one after the other down the row. They crackled and plumed, whooshed, and flared, our own Krakatoa erupting. For a moment, I thought I had been transported to the other side of the world, and now teetered on the lip of an active volcano.

I stepped back, instinctively protecting my Brownie behind my back. So close to the fire's nucleus, my senses heightened. My nostrils flared from the stench of seared wire. My eardrums popped. I could taste disaster, oily and bitter. My eyes focused on the tiniest images, single embers. The temperature of the fire oppressed my skin, even through layers of clothing. I felt on fire.

Extreme heat melted the steamer truck and incinerated a wooden cart. A fire horse, still hitched, was scorched on his right hind leg. Unharnessed agony set in. He spewed angry steam, pulling the team and the fire apparatus he was towing in a tight circle to walk off the pain.

"Goliath," called the hostler, who rushed to his side. "Goliath, easy boy. Take it easy."

The door behind me burst open and out flew several employees of Sol Ginsburg & Co. I stepped aside as staff of the menswear manufacturer, who worked on Sundays in order to observe their Sabbath, carried out accounting ledgers, cash boxes and bolts of fabric, along with shouts of "Hurry," "Run" and "This Way." I spotted Mr. Ginsburg and hoped he hadn't seen me. I knew him; he personally tailored Papa's suits. But there was no place to hide.

"Miss Anna, what are you doing here? Are you hurt?"

"No, Mr. Ginsburg. I'm fine."

"You mustn't stay here. This fire is too dangerous. And the wind could make it so much worse. Go home. Quickly."

"I don't want to leave."

Mr. Ginsburg looked aghast. "But you must."

I turned my back on him and glanced over my shoulder. An employee grabbed the arm of his boss and pulled him away. As he faded into the cacophony, Mr. Ginsburg's voice trailed behind.

"Go home, Miss Anna, please. Go home, before it's too late."

I faced him and, feeling no such urgency, shook my head defiantly. It was impolite, under any circumstance. Mr. Ginsburg was trying to protect me. And I disallowed him. But I wanted to know more, see more, and experience more of what I felt deep inside would be both historic and catastrophic.

A striking, familiar sound cut through the rage and din, a reminder of a promise made and, in all the fracas, forgotten. Church bells. They rang a call to prayer, most likely at St. Alphonsus.

Must be eleven o'clock, I thought. *Eleven o'clock! Is Adrian still waiting at the church for me? Does he think I jilted him? Surely, he must be sick with worry.*

My thoughts ricocheted right back to the unfolding drama when someone yelled that the fire chief had arrived. A stern-looking man in his fifties, wearing round wire-rimmed glasses, stepped out of a one-horse buggy, typical transportation to a fire for the chief.

George Horton, a dyed-in-the-wool firefighter, recognized the colossus facing him. He asked the city's 5th District Engineer, Levin Burkhardt, for an update on the blaze that now engulfed seven multi-story buildings flanking several main thoroughfares and two fire engines.

"Sir, between the wind and the tight quarters, this fire is going to spread fast. We need all the help we can get."

"In that case, I'm calling in the entire Baltimore City Fire Department."

He sent the Secretary to the Board of Fire Commissioners, Pinkney Wilkinson, to sound the tocsin.

I realized my safety might be in jeopardy and my presence would only impede the work these brave men had to do. Stepping into a narrow alley, I weighed the decision to stay or go. All the while, pictures of Adrian muddled my mind, along with the crush of overlapping voices all around.

It was impossible to think clearly. The fire activity threatened to destroy any rationality, no matter how hard I tried to discern what was most prudent. After a lockstep childhood, I found the unexpected completely overpowering.

Firefighters converged in no time, bringing all manner of equipment—steamers; ladder trucks; and combination engines, their tillermen having trouble steering around the mess. I had to get out of the way. With decision made, just as I started to head back to church, a hot trolley wire fell and struck Chief Horton on his leather helmet not more than ten feet from me.

I gasped and felt faint, then pulled myself together by pinching the loose skin between my thumb and forefinger. Hard. It hurt. It had become my habit to perform this painful ritual whenever I needed to be jolted out of the state Papa referred to as "perturbed."

Control your emotions or they will control you.

I could hear my father begin one of his long talks when temper or nervousness or even sadness overtook me. Instead of a lecture, a simple hug from Papa would have sufficed in uplifting my spirits and squaring the bond between us.

I drew a deep breath and composed my next shot, centered on the fallen fire chief and the men helping him. Somehow, I remembered to pause and wind the key on my camera to the next frame.

After clicking the shutter, I thought I had better start documenting the shots. I grabbed a piece of paper one of the Ginsburg employees had dropped. Pulling the pencil out of my fan pocket, I scribbled:

Roll 1, Frame 1 – 10:55am Firemen arrive at Hurst
Roll 1, Frame 2 – 11:15am Fire Chief struck

I became absorbed in my work. My *work*. It seemed rather strange. This was the only real work I had ever accomplished. Even though most women of high social standing did not hold jobs and earn wages, they filled their days with charity functions through women's organizations and church groups. Mothers tended to bring their daughters into this occupation with careful tutelage. I had been denied that bonding experience. It left me alienated from most young women my age and their mothers, and so-called "women's work." As a result, I could claim few friends.

At that moment, I felt purposeful. I heard a loud and clear call to action. My inner bells tolled. The person I was meant to be came into focus.

Then a small tug at my heartstrings begged for attention.

"Adrian!" I shouted.

I had completely forgotten about Adrian... again. I forgot that these two frames should have been pictures of our wedding day. How could I have lost track of my own life?

My reflection stared back in the remains of a storefront window. How dissimilar I looked from just an hour before in my bedroom. I wondered what my groom would think of me this way... scraped, disheveled, and smudged with soot. I wondered how Papa would regard me, behaving none like the daughter of a reputable doctor.

Before I could speculate any further, my eyes were diverted to something moving in the street. There, just a few feet away, orange embers reached out and snatched my leather gloves from the gutter. Slowly, they eased into each hand, finger by finger, a perfect fit, and transformed them into a melted wad of my former life.

CHAPTER 6

ADRIAN

Sunday, 10:50am

I wrapped the handkerchief around my knee and tied it tightly to stem the bleeding. It wouldn't stop. Blood pooled in my shoes and red stains rippled on the leg of my pants. It seemed that all of my hopes and dreams were flowing out of me. Sam caught up with me and offered help and support.

"I live just beyond the Shot Tower in Jonestown. We can make it there if we take it slow and easy," he said. "I'm certain my wife will be able to treat your leg."

Grateful for my co-worker's kindness, I limped along, leaning on Sam, with the wind at our backs, guiding us away from the fire. And Anna.

We passed the iconic Phoenix Shot Tower, once the tallest structure in the country. Now a dinosaur, it no longer produced shot for cannons and firearms. A kinship with how it once worked took hold. My anxiety hissed like molten lead hitting cold water, forming a solid ball of fear in my stomach.

Hordes of people rushed all around. As many as ran away from the fire ran towards it. People hurried all over the place, moving in circles, it seemed. The pandemonium, no more than an ant colony swarming a crust of bread. In the middle of it, I agonized... feeling lost, insignificant, helpless.

When we got to the apartment, Sam's wife, Lillian, took great care in tending to me.

"Are you trained, Lillian?" I asked. "You seem to know exactly what to do."

"My mother was a Civil War nurse. She experienced immeasurable suffering that plagued her with nightmares, bad memories she couldn't erase. She passed away two years ago."

"I'm sorry."

"I pray she found her reward. Thank heavens she taught me what she knew, so I can take care of my own family's needs. Doctors are expensive, you know."

"You honor your mother well."

"Thank you. That's kind of you to say."

Lillian had a gentle, shy way about her, even when applying pressure to the wound. She seemed embarrassed to be touching the bare leg of a strange man, even though her husband stood right beside her. After a few minutes, Lillian got the bleeding to stop. Without raising her eyes or conferring with Sam, she spoke to me softly.

"I think, in this case, you do need a doctor. Your cut is pretty deep."

Sam agreed. "I can get you to the hospital on the streetcar. It isn't very far."

Not for a moment did I want to go. I didn't care to explain why. My only desire was to be with Anna. This day should have been unfolding as planned. Anna and I should have been married by now. We should have been huddled on the streetcar, holding hands, staring at our rings, heading to our wedding bed in Canton... happy, nervous, dreaming, planning, loving. We should have been looking forward to our two-day wedding trip in the nation's capital.

I realized I would never be able to get to Anna unless I took care of myself. So, I agreed to go to the hospital with Sam. As we headed out...

Boom!

...we heard an explosion, followed by a loud rumble that rolled towards us like a runaway boulder on a steep slope.

"What was that?" I asked.

"I don't know, but it couldn't have been good," Sam replied.

"Sam, I need to get to the fire."

"Never mind that now, Adrian. Here comes the trolley."

On the short ride to the hospital, I perused the sky as it darkened with febrile circles of smoke, and flames spurted above mountainous buildings.

The fire seemed so close, too close to Anna's neighborhood. Fear rendered me deaf and mute. Beads of sweat lined my upper lip and dotted my forehead. The cheap band inside my hat wicked some of the droplets, while errant ones chiseled lines of worry in my face. I must have appeared as aged as a weathered stone sculpture.

"Adrian, are you all right?" Sam asked. "You look grey, like you're about to pass out. Adrian?"

Rudely, I didn't answer, so lost in thoughts of Anna and our wedding that I realized wouldn't happen that day. I never intended such unhandsome behavior on my part.

"Hold on, Adrian. We're almost there."

Distress oozed from every pore. Sam put his arm around me. He couldn't have known why I was so upset. God bless him. He stayed close to me anyway. A truer friend did not exist.

Once inside the hospital, I got immediate attention. My wound was sutured and dressed. Crutches were given to me, along with tincture of laudanum and instructions to take four drachms before climbing into bed at home. The doctor warned me that the drug was powerful; it would make me drowsy and could skew my thinking. I might even hallucinate. I was ordered to stay off my feet for the better part of four days.

What could I say? I had to agree, knowing how impossible it would be to follow orders. Disconsolate, I turned a corner in the maze of hospital corridors and came face to face with... Dr. Bainbridge. Too stunned to speak, I locked eyes with Anna's father.

"What happened? Is Anna with you? She better not be," the doctor said.

"I was alone when I was injured, sir. Anna was nowhere near," I replied.

Satisfied, the doctor started to step aside, then added, "Did you get proper care? Are you all right?"

"I will be," I replied. I really wanted to say, "I will be, as soon as I find Anna."

"Very well," Dr. Bainbridge said, continuing down the hallway.

"What was that conversation about, and who is Anna, if you don't mind me asking?" Sam said.

"Not now," I whispered.

Sam assumed I would want to go home, far away from the fire. He thought I would be more comfortable recuperating in my own bed and having access to a change of clothing and personal toiletries. He asked if I had any family who could take care of me. Surprised to find no one, Sam said he'd wait with me until the trolley arrived to return me home to my tiny apartment in Canton.

"I can't go there, Sam," I said.

"Why not?" Sam asked. "You heard the doctor's orders. You have to rest for four days. Are you worried about being so far from work? You can't deliver the mail in your condition anyway. And right now, the fire is destroying your route. I'll tell the foreman what happened. I'm sure he'll understand."

"I can't go home, Sam. I just can't."

"Adrian, what's wrong? Tell me. Come home with me and tell me what's troubling you."

I acquiesced and together we boarded the trolley. But no words were spoken.

As the streetcar clacked along, the blocks rolled by like a flip card movie. The rhythmic sound and motion lulled me into a daydream. A movie of my own played back in my mind. It started on one of those days when the cares of the world seemed to drift away like childhood bubbles through a clay pipe.

I was enjoying a petal-soft morning that showed no promise of romance. While taking a stroll through Patterson Park not far from home, I spotted Anna, the young woman who had caught my eye months before but hadn't reciprocated my advances. She was alone, taking pictures of the Victorian pagoda that stood on Hampstead Hill at the tip of the park. The two of us hadn't spoken since that first unsuccessful meeting on her doorstep.

As Anna looked down into the viewfinder of her Brownie, I stepped into her shot, bent low, stared into that tiny eye, and flashed my warmest smile. Anna waved me off.

"Do you mind? You're in my picture."

"That's exactly where I want to be."

"What do you mean?"

Despite Anna's curtness, I introduced myself formally.

"I've seen you somewhere before. Just a minute... you're the letter carrier in my neighborhood."

"Yes, and I see you purchased one of those Brownie box cameras. I delivered the advertisement flyer to you."

"You did?"

I could tell Anna was impressed with my memory. Of all the mail I delivered over so many blocks, over those months, that piece of paper had stood out. But she didn't say so.

"I'm sorry. I don't remember receiving the flyer from you, just getting my hands on this camera."

Then why did she remember me at all? Was she amusing herself? Anna fiddled with the camera and started to move away, so I diverted her attention.

"I was about to climb to the top of the pagoda. The view is a sight to behold. Might even make a nice picture. I hope this doesn't sound improper but, would you care to join me?"

Anna's eyes floated inside her head like a butterfly not knowing where to light. I held my breath until she answered. "Well, I guess I'll go with you. I really wanted to go up with my Papa, but he would never do it, no matter how many times I asked."

"Then, allow me to lead the way."

We circled the stairs until we couldn't go any higher and stepped out onto the balcony that wrapped around the structure. The view stretched wide over the park and surrounding neighborhoods. What a breathtaking sight from any angle... for us, made all the better shared. The smile spreading on Anna's face paid dividends on my investment of patient waiting.

"Why is there a pagoda here? Do you know, Adrian?"

"Yes, I do. This is Hampstead Hill, the site of a key standoff in the War of 1812. It was here that a naval brigade stood watch over the harbor, Fort McHenry and North Point. The information they gathered and the artillery and manpower they displayed helped crush the British. Their efforts proved to be a turning point in the war.

"You sound like you're quoting from a book."

"I read all the time, especially history books. It's important to know what came before. Have you ever seen Fort McHenry?"

"I'm afraid not. Might you take me?"

"I'd be delighted to be your guide."

For an instant, our eyes met with the understanding that this moment would recast our futures. Anna broke our gaze.

"But, why a pagoda? Why here?"

"It's just a decorative observatory. It was designed to bring Victorian charm to a battle entrenchment. I think it holds the possibility of success against all odds." I resisted saying, "It's a romantic place, a place to dream about life's unexpected good fortune, a place for strangers to fall in love." My true feelings had to be kept close to the vest for now.

Of course, we knew little about each other this early in our relationship. We were just two people, high above the world, looking out over our city, dressed in all its late summer frippery. But it seemed to me that, just as a bud unfurls, moving too slowly for the eye to discern, Anna was ever so slightly opening up to me.

More than anything, I wanted to hold Anna's hand; I didn't dare. I really wanted to kiss her. It was too soon and too forward a gesture, even though I had waited so long for this opportunity. I didn't want to scare her away, so I bided my time once again. Just the same, I sensed something welcoming in how close Anna stood to me.

Balancing on tiptoes, she stretched her neck to see as far as possible, her fingertips pressed to the railing for support. I started to whistle *I Can't Tell You Why I Love You/But I Do,* not knowing if Anna had ever heard the lyrics, all the while hoping she had and would get the message. She offered no indication, too caught up in composing photographs. I reached out and took her by the elbow to steady her. She didn't protest. I knew then and there that I would win her heart. I thought she knew it, too, because the corners of her mouth curled into the smile of one allowing herself to be beguiled. There would be no battle. This stand on Hampstead Hill would prove to be the turning point in our lives.

I relived our courtship and how happy we were when we were together. And reminisced about how I had opened Anna's world, with musicals at Ford's Theater on West Fayette Street;

skating in the park; and trips to the Baltimore Zoo, where Anna loved taking pictures of the lanky cranes. We visited music stores so I could learn new songs and memorize the lyrics from sheet music I wouldn't have to buy and couldn't afford anyway. Anna didn't sing well, so she accompanied me with the tapping of her feet.

It was soon made obvious how important I had become in Anna's life. She hadn't at all been shy about telling me so but it wouldn't have mattered anyway. Her camera spoke for her.

Anna rarely let go of her Brownie, as important a part of her as her own eyes. Sometimes, she would ask a total stranger to take a picture of the two of us enjoying ice cream cones or hot dogs, always cheek-to-cheek. Just the idea that Anna wanted to be paired with me in a photograph expressed more than her words alone could ever convey.

Jolted back to reality by an unruly child sitting behind me, I wondered when I would touch Anna's face again. Finding her consumed my thoughts until the trolley slowed, and my sweet memories came to a cold, clanging stop.

Once back at Sam's place, the two of us were greeted with a tray of coffee and scones with clotted cream and jam.

"Please take some refreshments," Lillian said.

Sam helped himself and offered me a plate, which I refused.

"Perhaps just some coffee then, to take off the chill?"

I made no reply. Lillian dosed my medicine and gave it to me. She looked at Sam, who hinted with a nod of the head that perhaps she should leave us alone. So she excused herself, saying she needed to tend to her baby, Lucy, in another room.

I had always been happy-go-lucky, the one cracking jokes and singing songs and making everyone smile. Now I was in need of cheering up. Sam had never seen me this way before. He was at a loss for what to do. He tried to humor me with one of my own riddles.

Sam sat beside me, waiting for me to say something. I merely stared straight ahead, as stone-faced as the statue of George Washington on Mount Vernon Square.

"Adrian, please talk to me. Tell me how I can help you."

Maybe the effects of the laudanum started to wear on my mind. I couldn't hold it in any longer. I took a deep breath and spilled the whole story quickly, everything about Anna and our planned elopement. And I revealed my innermost apprehensions concerning the fire.

"I want you to stay with us, Adrian. You shouldn't be left alone."

"I can't do that, Sam. I have to find Anna."

"You're not fit for such strenuous activity right now."

"I know, but what else can I do?"

"Just relax, everything will work out fine, I'm sure."

I grabbed Sam by the arm and wouldn't let go.

"Will you do me a favor, Sam? Go to the fire for me. See where it is. Go to the church. Ask the monsignor about Anna. I'll give you Anna's address. Go there, too. Look for her yourself. She's tiny, wears dark clothing. She'll be carrying her camera. You have to find her and tell me what's happened. Tell me she's safe. Please, Sam, help ease my mind."

"Well, umm, sure, Adrian. I'll go. I'll go right away. You stay here. Let the medicine do its work. I'll tell Lillian I'm... I'm running an errand for you, okay?"

Sam hemmed and hawed because he didn't want to go for anything. He had a wife and child and home to protect. How could I ask him to leave them and walk right into the infernal depths of a city afire? I was that desperate, is all I can say. Sam's generosity in agreeing to go humbled me.

"Thank you for doing this, Sam."

"I'll see to everything. I'll find Anna."

I watched as Sam slowly buttoned his overcoat and went on his way. Then, my thoughts drifted to chocolate cake and fragrant snowdrops and their sweet smells mingling and wafting through my empty apartment, wandering into the bedroom, searching for newlyweds, and nestling on the pale pink chenille covers that no one would be turning down anytime soon. Finally, I rested my head in the worn crook of a high-back chair and fell into a death-like sleep that only exhaustion laced with painkillers can induce.

CHAPTER 7

ANNA

Sunday, 11:30am

Bricks started falling. People ran for their lives. More buildings now burned out of control, the flames prodigious and spreading northeasterly. I moved in tandem with the conflagration like its identical twin.

By this time, word of the fire had reached the headquarters of the St. Paul Street Telephone Exchange, where forty operators sat at their switchboards, servicing most of the 14,000 phones in Baltimore. While the fire rampaged only blocks away, the women calmly fulfilled requests from police and firemen to call in more emergency workers. They helped to quiet frantic civilians on the other end of the line, who were worried about the fire... even the operators' parents, begging them to abandon their posts and come home. Every single operator remained loyal to her employer as all lines lit up continuously. Soon, business owners phoned, wanting their workers on the spot to help remove company records, office supplies and equipment. Hospitals requested staff to report immediately. No one answered the call of duty more unfailingly than the operators.

At 11:40am, Washington, D.C.'s Fire Chief W.T. Belt was telegraphed for help. The message simply, boldly read:

"BIG FIRE HERE. MUST HAVE HELP AT ONCE."

Baltimore raged and the inferno couldn't be contained from within its own ranks, no matter how well-numbered and skilled.

After Chief Horton was taken home to his sickbed, temporarily incapacitated, District Engineer Burkhardt stepped in and took command until the mayor arrived. Once he got there, however, it didn't make much difference.

Only thirty-five, Robert McLane held the distinction of being Baltimore's youngest mayor. The son of wealth and prestige, he was a competent politician. But with little experience in disaster, he found himself in the midst of one that threatened the very city he had sworn to serve. Without the help of Chief Horton, he had no idea how to attack this blaze. He and Burkhardt didn't think to set up a command center or a system of communication. How could they? A fire of this magnitude was inconceivable. The men merely ran from block to block, yelling short-term orders, along with words of encouragement.

Overwhelmed by the enormity of the fire and their responsibility to contain it, they must have been eager for D.C. fire companies to bring not only manpower and equipment, but also moral support.

The blaze took over the corners of Fayette and Charles.

Boom!

A second explosion fractured the sky. I ducked as shards of expensive crystal and china from J.W. Putts & Co., better known as the "Glass Palace," pierced the intersection. The fire catapulted from there.

It moved straight down Fayette Street with its sights set on three of Baltimore's most important landmarks—The Courthouse, City Hall and the Main Post Office.

In its path... Mullin's Hotel. The fire exhibited no restraint. Gluttonous as it was, it swallowed the building whole. I took a picture as the hotel disappeared in half an hour, then wrote in my log:

Roll 1, Frame 3 – Noon Mullin's Hotel fire

I backed away as the intensity of heat irritated my throat. A wheeze billowed into a cough so violent I lost my balance. A firm hand steadied me from behind, making my thoughts run to Adrian.

When I turned around, I saw a young man with light brown hair parted straight down the center, each side lacquered against his scalp. He stared back with sleepy, deep blue eyes that were both friendly and admonishing. Around his mouth curled a general expression of distaste. His ears stuck out too big for his head and his shirt collar and tie knot overwhelmed his neck. The most noticeable thing about this man was the lit cigar in his left hand, at which I stared in surprise. I couldn't help but comment.

"You're smoking during a fire... isn't that rather absurd?"

"Well, you're taking pictures. There is nothing more absurd than that. Shouldn't you be somewhere safe?"

"It's just that it's a bit of a shock seeing you puffing on tobacco, when you're already surrounded by smoke."

"It's an equal shock to see a girl risking her life for no good reason. Why are you doing it?"

"Umm, I'm not quite sure. When I saw the fire, I knew—"

"...you had to be here. You had to be in the middle of everything."

"You make it sound like I'm nothing more than an old busybody."

"Calm down. We're on the same side. There's enough ado on this day of rest for both of us."

"So, where's your camera, Mr. Kodak?" I chided.

"I'm a journalist. I write stories."

"For a newspaper?"

"I'm the City Editor of *The Baltimore Evening Herald.*"

"You are?"

"My name is H.L. Mencken."

"I'm Anna Bainbridge. I read your newspaper every day."

"Oh, do you?"

"Yes, I do. Are you challenging me? Do you think I'm lying?"

"I must say, you look awfully young to—"

"Would you like me to paraphrase the article you wrote two days ago on Attorney General Whyte's chances of making the Senate?"

"Well, that won't be necessary. I'm duly impressed. Now, what have you been photographing with that little camera of yours? Anything I should know about?"

I told Mencken everything I had experienced and showed him what I had written on my log sheet.

"Hmm," he said.

"What's the matter?"

"Well, if you want to be a photojournalist, you have to collect more information than this."

"What do you mean? Wait just a minute. How dare you presume to know me? Who said I want to be a photojournalist?"

"Oh, you do. Trust me. Or you wouldn't be here. If you have any hope of getting these pictures published, you have to know the names of all the main subjects in each shot. What fire company is in frame one? Who's the fire chief in frame two? I know his name but you don't mention it here. Is anyone else in the picture with him? Who are they? And you don't list the address of Mullin's Hotel. Was anyone hurt there? Are all the residents accounted for? This information is important. You say you read my newspaper but I doubt you really understand it. Haven't you ever noticed captions identifying the people and locations in the pictures? How do you think the paper gets that information? The photographers, writers and editors all have to work together."

"Say, I'm new at this. You don't have to be so rude."

"When you're reporting a story, you have to get answers to specific questions. What happened? Who was involved? When? Where? How did it unfold? You've listed the time each event occurred but not much else. You can't just take pictures. You have to ask questions and write down exact quotes and, most important of all, get confirmation from different sources. That's how you learn the truth. But I shouldn't expect so much from you. You're just a child, and a female to boot."

"Now, you listen here. You can't talk to me like that."

"Where's *your* camera, Mr. Kodak?" he mocked. "Don't chastise me when your own manners fall short of stellar. I'll talk to you any way I like. You'd better straighten up fast and dance on your toes from now on. This story is everblooming. What an enchanting opportunity stands before us!"

Even though I knew Mencken was right, I was offended by his attitude. Sputtering a curt "Goodbye," I turned to follow the fire, more so to hide my bruised ego. I wasn't used to taking the same kind of straight talk I so freely dished out.

"Don't you even want to know where *The Herald* is located? The corner of St. Paul and Fayette," Mencken yelled. "Write that down. You can't miss it. It has fireproof metal shutters on all the windows. It won't burn, I assure you. My office is on the fifth floor."

I kept right on walking, storming away, actually. So annoyed with that arrogant city editor, I didn't stop myself from wiping a tear on the sleeve of my best coat. After a few blocks, I slowed, eventually coming to a complete stop.

Distance couldn't separate me from Mencken's harsh words. But something he had said began to mollify my emotions.

A photojournalist... he called me a photojournalist, I thought. *Is that what I am?*

I started asking questions. Amending the log of pictures, I jotted down the name of the fire chief and added the cross streets where Mullin's Hotel once stood. I vowed to be more vigilant and thorough in gathering information. I grew more committed than ever, despite H.L. Mencken's slight.

I, Anna Bainbridge, was a "photojournalist."

Battalions from Washington had arrived and joined forces, their journey taking a speedy, unprecedented thirty-eight minutes. Volunteer firefighters from elsewhere in Maryland had also taken up position, and all were welcomed by their Baltimore brothers. Together, they improved the odds of beating the fire and, no doubt, saving any number of lives.

I minded everything, walking from street to street, poking around, searching for answers to questions, and taking notes to go with the pictures I shot.

After a while, I came upon a group of firefighters huddled around a hydrant. They tried repeatedly, without success, to connect the hose from a Washington fire truck. I had to communicate with them above the deafening roar of the fire.

"What's the matter?" I hollered.

Surprised to see such a bold young lady in the midst of the fire prying into their work, the firemen ordered me to back away. I badgered them until they were sick of me, insisting I was gathering information to give to *The Herald*, insisting that what they had to say was vitally important, until they had to respond.

"Our hose couplings don't fit your hydrants."

"What does that mean?"

"We can't tap into the water system. We can't help fight the fire."

I carefully wrote what the fireman said verbatim and repeated it to confirm my memory.

A lieutenant ordered someone to find rags, store awnings, and pieces of anything they could tie around the coupling to secure it and prevent leaks. When they finished, water poured through the hose nozzle but the pressure ran low. And without full force, they couldn't douse much higher than the second story. The firemen did the best they could, working together, despite the problem. Unbeknownst to them, this scene repeated at hydrant after hydrant across the fire scene. The fire knew it, though, and as a show of resolve, it rolled up some fireballs and bounced them from rooftop to rooftop, far out of reach.

By now, the blaze fully engulfed several blocks. Calls went out to fire departments in Western Maryland, Wilmington, Philadelphia and New York.

Local authorities changed their strategy. They ordered dynamite to create firebreaks. Later, when the supplies arrived from Anne Arundel County, they detonated the John Deur and Son building, already ablaze on German Street. That plan backfired. The dynamite blew out windows but the warp and woof staunchly remained and continued to burn. The blast also blew out several windows in nearby buildings untouched by the fire, giving grand entry to the flames. Within minutes of detonation, the entire fire doubled in scope.

Soon, flames practically licked the cornerstones of City Hall and the Main Post Office. When I arrived there, a police officer ordered me behind one of the many wooden barriers being erected to control the growing crowd of onlookers. I pushed through bankers, executives, and office workers, who had rushed downtown from outlying neighborhoods to check on their businesses. Finally, I fought my way to the front, where hundreds of other spectators also lined up just to see, with their own eyes, what hell on earth really looked like.

CHAPTER 8

SAM

Sunday, 1pm

I circled around the fire to the southwest and headed up Liberty Street. As I got closer, the temperature struck me as frigid and feverish, the air viscous and grey. Once or twice I became disoriented on streets I was used to walking every day. I had to take my time and step carefully around downed electrical wires, patches of ice, and indistinct debris piled up like a slag heap.

When I got near to where the fire had started, I was stunned to see mere facades of buildings, seemingly held erect by nothing more than icicles created by cascading water from fire hoses. They towered like pearly stalactites that had taken centuries to form in underground caves, making the city look otherworldly, prehistoric. Sagging electrical lines, weighed down with thousands of hair-thin icicles, gave the illusion of a fur coat's outstretched arms.

Whole city blocks had been wiped off the map. Fallen wreckage still smoldered on the ground with embers lying in wait, hoping to grab a passing pant leg or frilly underskirt. Firebrand, horse dung, and piles of bricks as tall as my sight line littered the streets. Business signs sat askew, swinging from stubborn nails that refused to give up the ghost. Huge pieces of mangled steel, resembling pulled taffy, cluttered the landscape. The milliner's shop had transformed into a morgue for mannequins.

"Looks like Baltimore is dying a slow, painful death from black lung, doesn't it?"

A tall, thin man spoke to me while sweeping the section of sidewalk that lined the width of his destroyed business.

"I beg your pardon?" I asked.

"My father was a coalminer all his life. It was a short one. When I saw what the mines did to him, I realized underground was not for me. Took me twenty years to build up my optician practice. Now, look in the window. All the wire frames have been soldered together. There's nothing left. It's as if the whole city were a coalmine. And we all have black lung."

"I'm very sorry," I said.

For the first time in my life, I saw men cry. I stood transfixed as owners and employees up and down the block held on to one another for comfort. Some sifted through charred stacks of bricks, wood chips, and daggers of broken glass. They searched for anything they could salvage, any physical evidence that they had once had a thriving business. All they found were the dregs of destruction.

I couldn't comprehend the heart-breaking truth these people were facing. Brokers. Lawyers. Merchants. Sweat shop workers. All reduced to the same pile of ashes, their faces frozen in deserted expression, their eyes the color of coal.

"I hope you can rebuild," I said, starting to walk away.

"Right now, I haven't the strength," the optician replied.

I pressed on towards St. Alphonsus, where every pew brimmed with worshippers holding an impromptu prayer service. The fire had swept within a few blocks of the Gothic revival church and left it alone. I dipped my fingers in the font, crossed myself, and thought of my mother's favorite saying. *One drop of holy water can quench the thirsty spirit and douse the devil's fiery breath.* I realized how true her words were.

Inside, no altar candles had been lit. Lighting of fire would have flown in the face of salvation. The dimness made the ornate sanctuary lose its eloquence and take on the graceful countenance of a saint spared martyrdom in the pyre.

"...but deliver us from evil."

After a quick prayer, I backed out of the church through the vestibule. The monsignor wouldn't be available to question for some time. So I decided to try the Bainbridge residence instead. Little did I know that Elizabeth, Anna's nanny and housekeeper, knelt in the front pew of the church, eyes closed, rosary in hand, praying for the safe delivery of the very person I was seeking.

I knocked and knocked, then went around the back of the house, opened the wooden gate to the tiny yard and pushed the servants' bell. No answer at Anna's home. I knocked on neighboring doors and pushed neighboring servants' bells, with the same silent reply. I thought maybe everyone had evacuated.

It was ungentlemanly to yell, but I had to exhaust every possibility of making contact with Anna.

"Hello, hello! Is anyone in the Bainbridge home?"

All I heard was the whistling wind.

At that point, the only choice was to follow the path of destruction directly into the heart of the fire. I wasn't quite sure what information there was to find, but knew I couldn't go back to Adrian without at least some morsel of hope to offer.

Nearing the north end of the fire scene, I saw several well-dressed people entering blazing buildings. They pushed past bystanders and moved with swift efficiency. Police were out in force, but there weren't enough to control the melee. Soon, these same people appeared in lower story windows and dropped things out... typewriters, chairs, tables, and small file cabinets. They were business owners, hoping to spare their livelihoods, all the while risking their lives. Employees standing in the street below rushed to pick up whatever didn't break.

"Can you help me?"

I looked up in the direction of a man's voice and said, "Who me?"

"Yes, can you grab this basket I'm lowering?"

The man tied a rope to the basket and started to ease it down from the second floor.

"What's in it?"

"A litter of puppies."

"What? How many?"

"Five."

"I'll bring the mother out. She's my dog and she had the pups a few days ago. She didn't survive. Must have taken in too much smoke while covering her babies. Maggie was a sweet girl."

"Oh, how sad."

I didn't want the responsibility but it had been put upon me. Before I knew it, the basket was even with my head. I settled it on the ground, untied the rope and peeked under the towel that covered the litter. Inside were tiny mutts that ranged from black to chocolate brown. One on top of the other, they squirmed for warmth and whimpered for a nipple. Despite the mother's loss, the sight of new life comforted me and made me hopeful in the midst of so much chaos and distress.

"Thank you, sir."

The man who had lowered the basket now stood by my side. I saw the pain in his eyes and the box in his arm, and wanted to turn away in disgust. He shook my hand and picked up the basket.

"I appreciate the help."

"Glad to oblige. I hope all the little ones survive."

Our friendly exchange was disrupted by a man running down the street, crashing into my shoulder. The jolt made me divert attention away from the poor soul with the puppies. I never saw him again.

Looters were mixing in with the crowd. Some were drunk, having been oblivious to the fire until they were chased out of all-night saloons by police. They broke storefront windows and made off with anything they could carry... housewares, clothing, even large shanks of meat. The man who had run into me carried a box of nails. Patrolmen made arrests but didn't know where to house the prisoners. They started carting those in custody to jails north and west of the city. The police chief had called for the National Guard to help restore order, along with undercover detectives, who would mingle among the crowds in search of pickpockets. It seemed even the behavior of normally polite people was growing rowdy fast, and needed controlling.

Regulation had dictated that police officers wear collars stiffened with celluloid. As a result, some caught fire. Several pulled out their stays right in front of me, momentarily stealing their attention from duty.

Hardware store owners were ordered to move dynamite, gunpowder and bullets off their shelves and as far away as possible. In front of one store sat four boxes of cartridges, snatched to safety in the nick of time.

"I want my money now."

"It's mine and I demand it."

"Give it to me, or I'll take it myself."

People who had money, wills and other important papers in safes appeared from all over the city while the owners of banks and storage businesses assured everyone that the depositories could withstand extreme temperatures if left airtight. Some people panicked and knocked down doors. They forced managers to open the locks. Braving intense heat that turned their skin to putty, they stood their ground. And when the safes were opened, all the bills and documents, every last one, crisped like fallen leaves and blew into the fire's thieving pockets.

I witnessed so much of it, too much. The magnitude of this swelling tragedy wore on me. My beloved Baltimore was quickly disappearing right before my eyes. I couldn't imagine the human, financial, and spiritual tolls this fire demanded. In what kind of world would my little baby, Lucy, grow up? I couldn't stand it anymore. And I couldn't stand seeing my own horror reflected in the faces of everyone around me. All I wanted to do was go home and be with my family, in case they, too, had to evacuate. I never asked for this assignment; it was thrust on me. But I had made a promise, so I persevered.

The chuffing of steamer fire trucks led me down Lexington Street, where a few blocks away a large crowd blocked my progress. Some had climbed fire escapes several stories high for a bird's-eye view of what was going on there. I stood behind the street crowd, some thirty deep, and strained my neck to see above them, only to find my own livelihood threatened.

Before me rose the Main Post Office, soon to fall victim. City Hall would be next. Other government buildings, like the Custom House, still under construction, stood in the fire's path. I feared little could be done about it.

I wormed my way through the masses. Something I spotted forced me into action... dozens of my coworkers positioned in long, orderly lines. They passed buckets of water from hand to hand, last to first and back again, doing what they could to douse the lower floors as a precaution, while firefighters tried to water down the roof and upper floors, all in an attempt to save the U.S. mail and this beautiful landmark.

Other postal workers pulled wagons and wheelbarrows filled with mailbags out the front door. I momentarily forgot about my family, Adrian and Anna. I had to join the brigade. Pushing through the rest of the crowd, I ran across the street past the barricades and police lines and stopped in my tracks. A flank of U.S. Army soldiers on horseback, with bayonets at the ready, circled the area. They had ridden three miles from Fort McHenry to stand guard and protect federal property. I ran around the building to get away from them; they were everywhere. A co-worker yelled, "Let that man through; he's one of us." The ranks parted and I slipped inside, my legs threatening to buckle in fear at any moment.

Entering the workroom, I looked around to see how I could be useful. The enormity of what had to be done overwhelmed me. I searched for a supervisor to tell me what to do. Someone else caught my eye first... hobbling on one crutch while trying to pull a heavy mailbag across the floor with his free hand.

"Adrian, what are you doing here?"

"Lillian scleamed," Adrian slurred his words, barely above a whisper. "I got outta bed. The flames... slo close to the Pose Office." He leaned heavily as if he had lost his other half.

"Come along, we're going home."

"The fire... the bluilding... so beauti."

"How did you get here?

"Black of a truck. Sam, help me. Save the mail."

"The only thing I'm going to save is you."

I left the room and returned with a small mail wagon.

"The foreman said I can take you home in this."

"No, Sam, we have to save the—"

"Come now, Adrian."

"Anna might ble in there... my parents. Save them."

"Adrian, the medicine is fiddling with your mind."

My friend teetered on delirium. His eyes had become glassy and unfixed, his breathing lacked rhythm, and his skin appeared chalky and moist. I took him by the arm to lead him away. Adrian resisted with more strength than I thought he possessed.

"Adrian, I am taking you back to my apartment right now, whether you like it or not."

The foreman helped force Adrian out of the building. We positioned him in a postal wagon. I pulled away and we were in motion before Adrian could protest any further.

All the way home, Adrian's words spilled out in a spiel of nonsense. He kept calling Anna's name, and the names of his parents, and said something about a wedding and a pagoda and cake.

When we reached my place, Adrian's expression looked as tenebrous as the smoke from the fire; he didn't even try to talk anymore. Lillian had to help me get him into bed. Just as we were about to leave the room, Adrian grabbed my arm and barely whispered, "Anna," before losing consciousness.

I felt compelled to tell my wife the whole story. I hoped Adrian wouldn't think I had betrayed his confidence. But Lillian needed to know. When I finished, she had only one thing to say as she slumped on the sofa.

"Mercy on us all."

CHAPTER 9

ANNA

Sunday, 3:00pm

My vision blurred and my eyes felt like they were being pricked with pins. They begged for rest from the brightness of flames and stinging of ash. My desire to stay with the fire became outweighed by the exigencies of life... discomfort, hunger pangs, and the need to relieve myself. As bad off as I was, I didn't want to return home. What could be said to my father when he asked where I had been? Would Adrian be there, too, having exposed our planned elopement? I wasn't ready for a piacular struggle that couldn't be won. Then, I remembered the bag of biscuits left in the confessional at St. Alphonsus.

I wended my way through the fire's onlookers and everyday guttersnipes. Before going into church, I tried the door to the parish school, which was always unlocked. Monsignor Vilkas once said, "God shuts out no one." This day was no exception. Inside, the usually teeming atmosphere was cold and empty. Since I had attended the school as a child, I knew my way to the bathroom and found it with minor difficulty.

When finished, I crossed the street and entered the church. Only a few people knelt there, muttering a novena, with each voice unique in its design, their susurrations as soft as falling snow, layering upon the next until all became one. The rhythmic monotone soothed my nerves.

I ducked into the confessional, sat on the kneeler, and reached into the bag for a biscuit. Then another. No meal this lean ever tasted so good. I ate greedily and reached for a third biscuit. But my fingers curled around a soft cloth and ribbon instead.

Stepping out of the confessional and into the dim light of the nave, I pulled a small parcel out of the bag. A pale blue cotton handkerchief with embroidered pink and white flowers held something hard edged like a rosary or necklace. The cloth was gathered up in a pouch tied with a white satin ribbon. This had to be a gift, no doubt, but from whom?

I sat in the back pew, released the bow, and unfurled the handkerchief in my lap. What I saw took my breath away.

"Elizabeth's chatelaine," I whispered. "And what's this... a sixpence?"

A folded note felt weighted by intrigue and fear. With hands atremble, I pried open its sharp corners. Fidgeting with the paper, I squinted to read its message. A blessing I was seated, because the handwritten words were stunning...

My dearest Anna,

You must forgive me. For weeks I have known of your plan to elope and lacked the courage to speak to you about it. I am not proud of the way I found out.

While tidying your room, a letter fell from a book on your bedside table. When I picked it up, I couldn't help but see the words "I love you" at the bottom. The handwriting was so bold I didn't need my spectacles to read it. And then, I couldn't resist reading the rest.

It was not my place to read your private missives but please understand, Anna. I did it because I care and am concerned about you. And, as your nanny, I'm responsible for your well-being. I helped raise you, and I only want what is best for you.

Before you fear being found out, let me assure you. I have spoken not a word of this to your father. Anna, what I am saying is, I approve.

Your happiness means everything to me. And after reading the note, I knew Adrian would make a good husband. By now you are married. May I be the first to congratulate you? Shall I call you Mrs. Crosby?

Anna, I want to present you with a wedding gift, however modest. I would much rather have given it to you in person but, under the circumstances, I knew I could not. This morning, I found a bag of biscuits on the bench by the door and I realized you were planning to take it with you. It was then that I slipped my offering inside, which I hope fulfills, in part, the poem...

Something old, something new

Something borrowed, something blue

And a silver sixpence in her shoe.

Anna, this is my chatelaine, the one you always admired. But the meaning of this gift runs so much deeper than that. I never told you... forgive me again... your mother gave it to me.

I stopped reading; this news bewildered me. All these years, I had lived under the impression that Elizabeth had come to our household *after* Mama died. And I felt a little angry with my nanny for not telling me otherwise sooner. Elizabeth knew how badly I wanted to learn everything about my mother. She knew that Papa always hesitated to answer any questions I had about her.

This letter proved admission of flagrant betrayal. I didn't want to finish it. Nonetheless, I took a deep breath and focused once again on the blotted ink.

The pain of not being able to tell you has burned a hole in my heart over these long years.

Anna, your father forbade me from ever revealing that I knew your dear, dear mother. I adored her. I adored you. I would have lost my position if I had said anything. And then I would have lost you both. I couldn't have withstood the pain. Someday, I will tell you everything about your mother. For now, your wedding is more important.

I love you as a daughter (if your mother will share you with me). I always have and always will.

Please accept this chatelaine that now connects the three of us forever.

Your faithful servant and nanny,

Elizabeth

I fingered the links of the chatelaine's chain with all the reverence due a rosary, and counted each attachment as if it held its own prayer.

I recalled, when just a child of ten or so, questioning Elizabeth about this strange piece of jewelry pinned to her apron.

"It's a chatelaine. That's French for 'lady of the castle.' The woman who runs the household uses it. In this house, that is my position. These implements help me get my work done."

Elizabeth unpinned the chatelaine and handed it to me. My eyes widened to inspect miniature scissors, a pince-nez, a sewing needle in its own sheath, a thimble, a tiny flat case containing thread, and a corkscrew, all linked together.

"The chain is sterling silver and the pin is centered on a pearl."

I rubbed my thumb over the repoussé design. It didn't take on a specific shape, like an animal or flower, posing more as an emblem, a coat of arms.

"I use all of these small tools when I clean the house. If I see a stray thread in the upholstery, I snip it with the scissors. I can mend a frayed curtain hem right away, without having to search for a sewing kit."

"And the glasses?"

"They're for my weak eyes when I thread a needle or sort the mail."

"And this thing?"

"It's a corkscrew. Sometimes your father wants me to open a bottle of sherry in his study."

"I think I'd like to clean a house someday, so I can have a chate-chate—"

"A chatelaine. Anna, I'm sure you will never have to clean a house a day in your life. But just the same, maybe someday I will give you this one when I no longer need it."

"I hope that day never comes."

"Whatever for? You just said..."

"Well, if you no longer need this, it means you're no longer our housekeeper and my nanny. I don't want that day to ever come."

Elizabeth wiped a tear with her apron.

Sitting in the church all those years later, tears of my own welled up. Maybe it was the biscuits, though it was more likely the filling up of the heart, but I felt content. The chaos outside encased me like a chrysalis, offering shelter from danger. For the moment, the church seemed far removed from the fire, Adrian, and our delayed marriage. I took off my hat, raised my legs up on the pew, lowered my head to be even with my feet, and rested. I caressed the chatelaine dangling from my fingers and thought, *It once touched Mama's hands.*

I felt a closeness to my mother I had never expected would arrive. A tiny tear rolled off my right cheek and blessed this precious gift. At peace amidst all the upheaval, I drifted off, and the dreams that visited me were very dear indeed.

CHAPTER 10

DR. BAINBRIDGE

Sunday, 3:00pm

My caseload overflowed. More and more casualties of the fire arrived at the hospital, some life threatening. A makeshift medical emergency center set up near Gay and Orleans Streets sent victims with various injuries. As a precaution, militiamen from the 4th and 5th Regiment Armories transferred some patients from City Hospital on St. Paul Street to my facility. The Lying-In Hospital of the Maternité of Maryland on West Lombard Street moved new mothers and babies.

Firefighters suffered singed palates, throats and lungs. Other people, ranging from police officers to onlookers came in with burns, smoke inhalation, heart arrhythmia, and anxiety. I helped stabilize patient after patient with my medical student by my side. I eased their pain, although I, myself, suffered.

Thoughts of Anna plagued me. *Had the fire reached home? Was Anna injured? Was she receiving help?*

Lord, help me. I did nothing to get these important questions answered. How much time would it have taken to send a messenger to my house? Why couldn't I have been bothered?

Even though my income well afforded a telephone, the idea seemed uncivilized. I abhorred the invasion of privacy it would have caused. But at this moment, how integral to my peace of mind a telephone could have been. How important in my ability to show Anna my concern.

I didn't even think back to another time, seventeen years earlier, when family should have been my priority and wasn't... and the price I paid for this unforgivable mistake.

With each new patient arrival, information about the fire trickled in, most of it inconsistent. I couldn't tell where the blaze had started and what path it had taken. Earlier in the day, when I had run into Adrian, I hadn't yet heard about the fire. I wondered if Anna's suitor had told me the truth. What really caused his injury? And more importantly, was Anna with him all along?

I banished these negative thoughts from my mind. The needs of the hospital precluded all else. There were tests to be performed, diagnoses to be made, and treatments to administer without let-up. And I held full responsibility for leading my staff through it all.

"Doctor Bainbridge, Doctor Bainbridge, please help us. Hurry!" a familiar voice cried.

At the end of the corridor stood Sol Ginsburg struggling to support a limp man. I ran to Sol's side and ordered the medical student to secure a gurney.

"Sol, what happened?"

"He just collapsed. He's one of my best tailors. He complained of pains in his chest. I think it was all too much for him."

Over the next couple of hours, I cared for several such patients. Finally spent, I dismissed the student, took a break, and wandered back to the ward where the clothier's employee lay sleeping. Sol sat in a chair nearby with his neck akimbo, about to nod off himself. When I touched his shoulder, Sol jumped and straightened in his seat. He immediately focused on the figure in the bed.

"He's doing better, Sol. He'll recover."

"Oh, Doctor Bainbridge, thank you. You are such a good man. How can I ever repay you?" He paused to take in the day's stress etched in my face and added, "You must be exhausted from all this."

"I am fine. You should go home and get proper rest yourself. I will take care of him."

"I think I will. I'm not as young as I used to be. Thank you again, Doctor."

"Before you go, Sol, tell me something. What do you know about the fire? Was it near your business?"

"It started right across the street in the Hurst building. It just exploded. Didn't your daughter tell you?"

"What do you mean?"

"I saw her there. She was taking pictures."

"Anna? In the middle of the fire?"

"Yes, sir. I urged her to go home but she seemed reluctant. The whole thing scared me to death but she didn't appear to be frightened at all. In all my life, I never saw anything like it. The fire happened so fast and with such power. My employees and I had to rush around, grabbing anything we could get out of the building. I'm an old man, Doctor, and what I carried was heavy. And the fire spread so quickly. I couldn't stay. I had to protect my staff and myself."

"Anna didn't go with you?"

"No, sir."

Leaving the room without saying goodbye, I ambled to the doctors' lounge, sat down, and feared my daughter might really be in trouble.

She was headstrong, I knew. But taking pictures of a massive fire? I couldn't imagine why she would put herself in such peril. What was wrong with Anna, and why was she causing me so much distress?

I remembered the Brownie camera my daughter had purchased the previous year. She loved using it so much, the camera had become an appendage. Now my blood ran cold as I imagined the danger she was imposing on herself just to get a photograph.

Why hadn't she grown up to be like Victoria?

Just thinking of my wife... and how she died... and my role in...

It all came flooding back, the grief, the guilt. These many years, I had tried so hard to bury my culpability under the burden of casework and medical breakthroughs and student development. Now it started to resurface.

I had idolized my wife. From the first time I met her, I observed her through a thin, amorphous veil of perfection. It made her appear angelic, flawless. I never saw Victoria as mortal flesh and blood.

This distorted view proved fatal.

She had been a rare rose, like the *Reine Victoria*, named for England's queen. My wife blushed the faintest shade of pink found in that flower, and her skin took on its gentle veining. The *Reine Victoria* so loved springtime that it bloomed profusely in honor of it. And that's the season when Victoria felt most alive, too. She would sit under the lilac trellis in the garden for hours, smiling as she breathed in all the fresh scents of earth's reawakening.

When the sun beamed down, Victoria protected her delicate skin with a white ruffled walking umbrella. By day, her honey-colored hair rested atop her head with pink satin ribbons woven through her chignon as if Mother Nature had placed them there. At night, when she let down her mane, it framed her heart-shaped face like a flower's corolla. Light green-brown eyes smiled when they alighted on anyone she loved. And she loved everyone. She floated rather than walked and when speaking, dulcet sounds wafted through the room with the nuance of rose water. Nothing but kind words ever crossed her lips. At least... that's how I saw her.

I adored Victoria but these uxorious feelings and expectations were not realistic. I have finally come to terms with it. I thought her too perfect to ever get sick, to ever succumb. And when she did get sick and did succumb, I became inconsolable. Why hadn't I, a doctor, recognized the symptoms of scarlet fever sooner? With so many people falling victim, why had I placed my wife above it all?

At first, I visited her grave daily and begged forgiveness, even though I admitted guilt to no one. I built a headstone fit for a queen, tall and stately like a door to the other side that might one day open and allow her back to earth. I'd sit by her grave and read, through watering eyes, the chiseled lines of my wife's favorite poem by William Wordsworth:

Our birth is but a sleep and a forgetting
The Soul that rises with us, our life's Star
Hath had elsewhere its setting
And cometh from afar.

Not in entire forgetfulness,
And not in utter nakedness,
But trailing clouds of glory do we come
From God, who is our home.

Try as I might, I never found comfort in those words.

After Victoria died, I no longer believed in God, or souls living forever, or the idea of heaven from which all came and would return. How could a loving God suffer my wife to such an ignoble fate and snatch the life from her so soon?

Over time, I visited the cemetery less often, just a few times a week, then one, until finally stopping altogether. Searing, unabated pain stood guard there and kept me away.

Gradually, I sloughed off any responsibility for my wife's suffering and death, and pushed the blame on the Almighty. Deep down, I knew. I knew the truth.

Without Victoria, I had become numb to beauty. My attitude so dishonored the way Victoria had lived her life.

She had been dedicated to the church and demonstrated her faith daily. She could often be found alone in a pew, praying her rosary with eyes transfixed or meditating on the Signs Of The Cross. Every week, she visited the sick and troubled members of the parish. She lifted their spirits and became their best medicine.

Victoria never blamed God or any mortal for the tragedies in life. She merely accepted whatever happened, both good and bad, as nothing more than God's will. *"Blind faith,"* a young Father Vilkas once called it.

Victoria's loving nature had flourished in the home life she created. She welcomed guests with warm embraces and graceful charm. She made them all feel so comfortable that they never wanted to leave. And that was just fine with her, and me, for that matter. We both loved to entertain. Teas and formal dinners went on for hours, with imaginative conversation, word games and decadent desserts, often leading into the parlor, where Victoria played Debussy and Chopin and sometimes hymns on the piano, to everyone's appreciation.

Laughter sang the most beautiful music, and it resounded throughout the house long after guests departed. Gaiety proved the perfect antidote to the stress that followed me home from the hospital. I couldn't get enough of the joy Victoria brought to my life. And I couldn't have loved her more.

I had been beside myself when my wife told me she was with child. I doted on her throughout the pregnancy, seeing that she had every convenience and indulgence. I needn't have worried. Victoria delivered Anna without complication and recovered quickly, her petite figure seemingly unaltered. Motherhood suited Victoria like springtime.

When Anna was but two, a wave of scarlet fever swept through Baltimore and Washington. Victoria was too delicate a flower to resist the strain. She withered and died within two weeks.

Through all of her agony, Victoria accepted her fate without a single waver of faith. *Blind faith, indeed*, I thought.

The epidemic killed so many people over a short period of time, officials couldn't keep an accurate head count. Several corpses had to be placed in single, mass graves to contain the spread of germs. Bodies of the poor were incinerated within hours of death. Being a doctor and a prominent member of society, I was one of the few people granted the privilege of holding a dignified church funeral and burial for my wife, however swift.

I mourned Victoria day and night until the pain made my own spirit curl and brown and crumble into ash. I might as well have been buried with her.

Music and laughter and light moved out of the house. Parties ceased. The keys of the grand piano in the parlor became stuck with dust and death. Victoria's refrain ended as abruptly as a staccato note. Years later, with what little hope I had left in my heart, I encouraged Anna to play, for no other reason than to resurrect my wife in some manner. In Anna, I found neither talent nor interest.

I saw little of Victoria in Anna. My daughter didn't even look like her mother, except in petite stature. Anna had brown hair and a plain face. She didn't float; she pranced. She paraded her unapologetic, tactless and mulish ways. Unkind words crossed her lips all too often. Sometimes she spoke her mind to the point of rudeness, without regret. As for her reputation, she didn't give a fig how others viewed her.

I didn't think Anna lacked merit, though. She possessed intelligence and knew her mind. She seemed determined, not frivolous like so many young girls. I had to respect that trait. She loved to be outside, as though the confinement of walls and windows and doors might inhibit her ability to breath. She faced the world with full sun on her cheeks, even though I tried my best to make her conform to Victoria's ways.

And Anna was curious, interested in everything happening around her. That was why she loved taking pictures. She once told me that photography accomplished the impossible. It froze time, as if a fleeting frame of life were suddenly tangible, able to be broken down and examined in minute detail. What happened too fast for the naked eye to discern, now existed forever, on film. Photography possessed all the qualities of microscopic discovery. She might have made a good doctor, had she been a man.

I knew Anna had a great deal of respect for the power of photography because the camera never lied. It told the truth, even if it hurt. And that's how Anna's inner workings were designed.

Anna could never be described as a flower; she grew more like a vine that runs wild, weaving in and out of earth and air, grabbing life with a tight coil. She proved rugged, indestructible, unforgiving. Some would even call her manly.

I loved my daughter because Victoria bore her, but more often than not, I resented her because she was not Victoria. There existed no thin, amorphous veil floating between father and daughter. In my disappointment, I often turned my back on her and focused even more attention on medicine.

A carapace formed around my soul. It grew and thickened, making it nearly impenetrable. Anna had to work hard to win my favor. The more she tried, the less she became her mother. The more she tried, the less she became a lady. The more she tried, the more she became someone I never wanted her to become. I need only look in the mirror to recognize that person, and see disapproval staring back like a fatal prognosis.

"Doctor Bainbridge, are you all right?"

A nurse sat down by my side, trying to make eye contact.

"We've been searching for you. You're needed right away."

"I'm sorry. I'll be there in just a moment," I replied.

As I walked back down the hall, I worried for Anna; at the same time, I trusted her ability to take care of herself.

Even though I hadn't set foot in a church since my wife's funeral, and even though I no longer believed in a Higher Power, I secretly prayed for Anna's safe return. I also prayed for the ability to tame my wild, wayward vine.

Almost immediately, I chastised myself for turning to God, an act I determined to be committed in a moment of weakness. Dismissing any unease, I got back to work and thought no more of deity or daughter.

CHAPTER 11

ANNA

Sunday, 6:00pm

While I rested at church, the phone exchange operators on St. Paul Street stayed on their lines. The blaze crept ever closer, forcing firefighters to douse the outside of their building so the women could continue their work. The heat of the fire broke windowpanes, while embers alighted on window sills like pigeons' feet. Finally, the women were ordered to cover their equipment and evacuate, but take their headpieces, in order to resume their posts as quickly as possible.

All the operators reached safety, opening umbrellas to deflect flying firebrand. Many tried to preserve their good shoes, stylish ones they had worked so hard to afford, by walking through the hot rubble in stockinged feet.

Within two hours, their building was gutted and unrecognizable. They would not get to plug in their headpieces again until the next day. At a different facility.

I never photographed that story because I had been sleeping, only learning of it elsewhere over the next couple of days.

I awoke to the sound of the church bell tolling, and became curious about what I had missed. I carelessly plopped on my bonnet and pinned Elizabeth's chatelaine to my coat. After finishing the biscuits with jam, my mouth became pasty with thirst and I felt like I had outgrown my clothes.

The swan-bill corset I wore dug into my ribs. The boning had been designed to tilt the pelvis back while thrusting the torso forward. It was supposed to create allure, making the wearer look as if she were leading with an "ample" bosom, while her "natural" bustle followed in a secondary search for attention. I never cared for such deception. Elizabeth and propriety had forced me to wear it. Failure to conform would have set the gossip hens flapping. What did I care at this point?

I stepped into the confessional, removed the underpinning and packed it in my suitcase, which I left behind again. Then my dress felt too tight. I pulled the miniature scissors from the chatelaine and snipped some of the stitches in the seams here and there. Free of any feminine constraint, I picked up my Brownie and exited through the vestibule.

The sun had already set. The dark sky hung like a wool blanket about to drop down and smother the stubborn flames. The temperature had plummeted to seventeen degrees. Thirty-five-mile-an-hour gusts blew. The wind hadn't spoken to me in a long time and wanted to remind me who had the upper hand. So a squall swooped in, stole my hat like a contemptible child, and threw it down an alley, where it rolled on its brim like a broken phonograph record, lifted off the ground, and caterwauled into the far reaches of night.

I became enraged. I wanted to chase down the wind and take back what was mine. People I could handle. But this? Never before had I been forced to battle the elements as if they were human. Fire. Cold. Wind. And now, the dark. It struck me that I would probably be out alone and unprotected all night.

Anna, stay focused on the task at hand.

Papa's words tapped me on the shoulder whenever I failed to complete one assignment before starting another. This time I listened, returning attention to documenting the fire.

For some strange reason, I had felt at home in the middle of all the action, even happy. Was there something wrong with me for feeling this way? I couldn't fathom why unfolding tragedy excited me so. Was this what it meant to be a journalist?

I looked down at my Brownie, useless in the dark. In mass production, Kodak had fixed the aperture on one setting that worked only in natural daylight. What would I do until dawn?

Curiosity energized my resolve. If I couldn't take pictures, the least I could do was find out what had transpired while I slept, and I knew just the person who could tell me.

Now, where did he say The Herald *was?*

With all the surrounding destruction and the fire burning beyond, I had trouble finding my bearings. I reached what I thought was the intersection that converged at H.L. Mencken's office building. In the darkness, amidst the entropy, I wasn't confident.

"Miss, what are you doing here?"

Out of the shadows, a man's face moved so close to mine that I could count each of his long, curly eyelashes.

"Is this the corner of St. Paul and Fayette?" I asked.

"Yes, miss, but you can't stay here. It's too dangerous for a young lady like you. You should go home, where you belong. Move away now."

"But... I work in this building... I'm... I'm an employee of *The Herald*," I lied. "I'm a photojournalist."

"I'm sorry. You have to leave. That's by order of the mayor, miss."

The man puffed his double-breasted chest, flaunting his badge.

"Can't you just look the other way this time?"

"Absolutely not. Now be a dutiful girl and go."

Reluctantly, I left. A block away, I stopped, shocked by my own lie, so out of character. My inner workings had somehow gone out of whack, like a metronome off a beat. Most bothering... the words had flowed right off my tongue as if I'd been lying a lifetime. I wanted to go back right away and set the record straight. Only, I didn't. Once down that road, I'd have to backtrack even further. The weight of all my recent transgressions sloped my shoulders and dampened my spirit.

I thought about the planned elopement and how running away had been an even worse lie. Withholding information, plotting behind Papa's back, sneaking out of the house. It was all one, big, ugly lie... of omission.

The guilt that silenced my tongue soon yielded to thirst when I spotted a seeping fire hydrant. Without thinking, I bent down and slurped as much water as I needed. The stream dripped down the side of my face into my free hand. Several clumps of curls that had fallen from their pins became drenched and stuck to my cheeks. I didn't think to pull out Elizabeth's handkerchief and dab my face in a ladylike manner. Instead, I wiped my chin on my coat sleeve and let ringlets of hair fall where they wanted.

The transformative power of the fire had taken hold of me, forcing me to shed the past. The molting process revealed a fresh undercoat I didn't recognize. I could no longer claim to be the privileged daughter of a cardiologist, living in a spacious, decorous home. Nor was I the fiancée of a man who couldn't wait to make me his wife. I had turned feral, slinking down alleys, scavenging for food and drink, searching for shelter, moving to the rhythms of the city and its own unique time signature.

For some reason, I thrived on it. This newly exposed skin was becoming, suiting me like Adrian's love had in the beginning. It seemed that the fire had swept me off my feet in much the same way as my groom.

From deep within my soul, a wave of knowing spread throughout my body. The feeling developed like a photograph; a sharp image materialized. I saw myself shooting pictures for a newspaper the rest of my life. I knew, in that moment, that I wanted to be a professional photojournalist. And no one could stop me. *Not Papa. Not even Adrian.*

I blushed over such a hostile thought, not so much concerning Papa. Rather, I felt guilty for thinking so ill of Adrian, for underestimating his commitment to my happiness. I thought he would never prevent me from doing anything I truly loved. Then doubt—that silent, slinking intruder—crept in and whispered, "Even this?"

How could I work in such a demanding career and still fulfill the duties of a wife and mother? Especially with the large family Adrian wanted more than anything. I had no answer, no role model.

As I continued along, lost in reverie, I stepped on a crumbled, water-stained sheet of paper resting on the cobblestones. Bending down, I read printed words slightly smeared across the top: "Come Down Anytime... A Good Time Is Promised." I choked as I picked up the paper that had once been as white as a brand new tablecloth. It was the menu from the Carrollton Hotel's first-floor restaurant.

That's where Adrian had proposed to me.

A swanky hotel, The Carrollton nearly took up an entire city block flanked by Baltimore and Light Streets. I had never dined at the Carrollton's restaurant before. Most times, I ate with Elizabeth in our kitchen because Papa took his meals alone at odd hours either in his study or at the hospital.

The formal dining room had not been used since Mama died. So I felt a rush of excitement when Adrian invited me to such an unusual, grown-up place.

It was late autumn. I had agreed to meet Adrian at the Carrollton. After joining him in the lobby, we rode up and down all five stories in the elevator several times, our giggles rising with each floor. Baltimore boasted responsibility for building the first electronic elevator that used a rotating drum to coil the hoisting rope. We were proud to be on one, especially since elevators were still a novelty to most people. We rode until we were dizzy and giddy and hungry for dinner.

"One more time, please, Adrian?"

"We'll miss dinner if we do. Let's eat, Anna. Then, we'll see how you feel."

We were seated at one of the many square tables. Tall, thick palms in ornate pots separated each one to ensure privacy. The tablecloths spread out soft and white, and the silverware sparkled like lovers' eyes. Hanging planters suspended far below the high ceiling. And Asian screens, opened in a zigzag pattern, elevated the dining experience to exotic.

I allowed myself to be swept up in the atmosphere. It made me feel mature, like a woman in love.

Adrian had ordered for both of us... the chef's house salad, filet du mignon au champagne, creamy mashed potatoes, and sparkling wine. Not wanting to appear unsophisticated, he pointed to the menu rather than mispronounce the French words. The dinner must have cost him two weeks' salary.

Over tea and cake, Adrian popped the question, taking me by surprise. I had not expected anyone to ever propose, and certainly had never thought Adrian would so early in our courtship. And without asking Papa first! It was scandalous and rebellious... and I loved it.

He began by smiling with the soft, delicate skin just below his eyes and above his cheekbones. His mouth curled and his bright blue eyes rippled like the lapping waters of Lake Montebello, one of our favorite places to stroll.

Without leading up to it at all, Adrian said, "Anna Bainbridge, will you do me the honor of becoming my bride?"

Adrian's words tasted sweet. Overcome with joy, I squealed above the polite conversations at adjoining tables. Adrian laughed heartily at my spontaneous reaction.

Embarrassed, not for myself, but for Adrian, I tried to compose my emotions but found it impossible. I clutched the cloth napkin to my lips and nodded emphatically, a delicious mixture of tears and laughter escaping.

Recalling the exhilaration of that moment, I missed Adrian with all my heart. I craved his gentlemanly hesitation in holding my hand and his long side glances when he didn't think I was aware of him. I missed the tiny love notes he tucked into the architrave of my front door when he delivered the mail... and the intrigue of leaving missives for him there, too. I pined for one of the songs he reserved only for me, and the sight of him walking towards me with one hand in his pocket, his step springing with all the energy and confidence of George M. Cohan. More than anything, I needed the way he made me feel, so loved, so respected, for the person I was. Adrian had never once tried to change me. Now I felt sick that I had forsaken a promise to meet him at St. Alphonsus and, instead, had chosen to follow my own impulses.

What else could I have done? This event was extraordinary, offering a once-in-a-lifetime opportunity. Adrian would understand. Wouldn't he?

Even though the menu was soiled, I rolled it into a cylinder and tucked it into my fan pocket. The hotel featured story-high windows with great views of the harbor. By now, those same windows must have been the hotel's downfall; they had to have blown out and allowed the fire in. The building probably had crumbled in ruins and I intended to hold on to this memento of my engagement to Adrian forever.

What a difference between the elegant feast we had enjoyed that night and what I had just consumed. In a few short months, I had gone from dining on steak, sipping wine from crystal stemware, and patting the corners of my lips with a pressed linen napkin... to eating biscuits and jam in a church confessional, gulping water from a fire hydrant, and mopping my mouth with a coat sleeve like a common street urchin.

I dwelled on what had become of me. I wrestled with the tug of my heartstrings and the pull of the fire within.

Was the lure of becoming a photojournalist growing stronger than my love for Adrian? I hoped the answer would come to me before I had to face my fiancé again.

Hope is lazy and useless without commitment and action.

I couldn't take any more of Papa's advice. I didn't need another enemy. My own warring thoughts were battle enough. I put him out of my mind and hurried my step.

In no time, I arrived at the foot of the fire on the east side of the city.

"There you are."

I searched the hordes of people to see where Adrian called to me.

"Over here."

"Oh, Mr. Mencken. It's you."

"Well, thank you for such a keen greeting."

"No, it's just that—"

"Never mind. Where have you been? What have you photographed?"

"Suppose you tell me what you've learned. I've been resting the last couple of hours."

"Resting? You can't rest at a time like this. Why, I was out last night until 3:30am, being pleasantly edified at Junker's Saloon, I must say. I'm here today with only a couple hours of sleep. You have no such excuse. Besides, I'm not telling you anything. You might take the information to *The Sun* or *The Baltimore American*, and where would that leave me?"

"Don't be ridicu—"

"I can't stand here idling with you. I need to get back to my office. If you want to talk, it will have to be on the way."

"But... but... the police won't let you—"

"Won't what?"

I couldn't keep pace; Mencken walked so fast. He moved in front of a police line and stepped right up to Mayor McLane to get a statement. He wrote notes as he walked and, when he reached his building, he strode straight past the same police officer who had stopped me earlier. The patrolman just tipped his cap in acknowledgment. It seemed to me that H.L. Mencken had the run of the city. He could go wherever he pleased and do whatever he wanted with complete impunity. I had to admire the power he possessed. I wanted to stay in close proximity to soak up as much of it as I could greedily store for myself.

"Well, are you coming?" he asked. "Well...?"

Heart... tug. Fire... pull.

I didn't want to be forced to take sides. I wondered if it could be possible to have two loves of equal weight. Why should one have to win over the other?

Mencken grew impatient. He turned his back on me, leaving me to feel subjugated, a raw reminder of the same tactic Papa often used to get me to do his bidding. The newspaperman opened the door to his building and entered.

I had to let go of my pride and all inner struggles, and allow my instincts to serve as a guide. For now, I gave in to the pull, reaching Mencken's side in seconds. It took even less time for all thoughts of Asian screens, and potted palms, and romantic dinners to blow away in the wind like a fine lady's broad-brimmed hat.

CHAPTER 12

ADRIAN

Sunday, 7:00pm

"Adrian, wake up. Adrian?"

The room was spinning; I had trouble making out the man speaking to me. He was as blurry as my view from the Human Roulette at Electric Park. I still felt groggy from the last dose of laudanum and had trouble adjusting.

"Wake up. We have to leave right now," Sam said.

"Wha... huh?"

"Here are your shoes and coat. Put them on. Get your crutches. Lillian has your medicine. Hurry."

I stumbled to my feet and got dressed in a drug-induced haze. Disoriented, I had to walk with Sam's help, while Lillian, who held little Lucy tightly, led the way out the door and down the steps to the street.

Nighttime had fallen, although now, so near the fire, the glow burned brighter than if the sun had been stoked with a poker.

For the moment, I thought I had not awakened to the real world at all. Rather, I had died, stood before a judgment I didn't remember, and was falling into eternal hell.

"Why? Why?" I kept muttering.

Sam misunderstood my question.

"The fire is getting too close. We have to leave."

Outside, Sam pulled out the post office wagon from under the wooden steps and settled me in it. He placed the crutches across my lap as if to strap me in. Lillian said she had everything she needed, and together we headed farther east, away from the fire. The cold air cleared my head and vision.

"Adrian, you said you lived in Canton. Can we stay at your place for now?"

"My place? No. My wife, Anna, will be there. It's our wedding night."

"I'm sorry to remind you of this, Adrian. The wedding never took place... because of the fire. Remember? Now, your address, please?"

"What? No."

After much prodding, Sam got the address out of me and we set out for Canton, a neighborhood named for Chinese exporters who, at one time, docked their ships nearby. Dozens of other people joined us in their slogging exodus.

"May we hop on your trolley?" Sam said to a conductor.

"I'm sorry, all the trolleys have lost their power, but we're required to stay with them when they are stranded. My wife said she would deliver meals to me for as long as it takes. I hope she comes soon. I'm hungry."

"We have no food to offer, I'm afraid," Sam said.

"That's all right. Don't try looking for a handsome cab either. All vehicles have been banned from the streets to allow the fire engines in. The only exceptions are men with buggies clearing debris or providing food to the firemen or delivering coal to the steamer fire trucks. That little wagon all you have?"

"Yes. We'll make do."

The bell at City Hall pealed at one-minute intervals. It sounded a call to the National Guard, signaling an urban riot. To us, it seemed more like a death knell. We walked faster.

The farther we got from the blaze, the colder the gale felt. Even though the wind blew at our backs, hastening the fire closer, we were glad for its help in pushing us ahead of the flames.

Bang!

Bang! Bang!

"What's that?" Lillian cried.

"Hurry!" Sam replied.

Behind us, authorities set off charges, intentionally dynamiting buildings, in an effort to give the fire nothing left to burn.

Sam and Lillian ran the last several blocks, lugging me all the way. I must have been such a burden. By the time we got to Canton, we were all breathless and panting, droplets of winter sweat bringing on the shivers.

"Adrian, where's your key?"

"My key? To what?"

"Your apartment. Come on, Adrian, please?"

Sam later apologized for rummaging through my winter coat, where he felt a key in a welt pocket. Unlocking the first-floor apartment door, he found flickering electricity when he pressed the cream-colored center of the round, black light switch. Lillian sat on the love seat to catch her breath and calm her crying daughter. Sam, so selfless, delayed his own comfort. He undressed me and gently eased my body into bed, its soft pink linens awaiting a bride. Too tired to mourn her absence, I gave in to the familiar feeling of my own comfortable nest.

Chapter 13

SAM

Sunday, 9:00pm

Within seconds, Adrian had fallen asleep again, but not before mumbling something about the wedding trip to Washington he thought he and Anna had already taken.

"Maybe he's hallucinating, Sam. Should we try to get him back to the hospital?"

"The doctor said the laudanum might have this effect. Let him sleep for now. I'll keep checking on him. You take care of Lucy."

Even though my wife and I quivered from the cold, we were hesitant to light the coal stove. The sight of fire, however warming, seemed unbearable. We were hungry, too, after such a long haul, especially once we spotted a chocolate cake on the kitchen counter. We didn't like helping ourselves to Adrian's food, but empty stomachs and the need for some kind of comfort got the better of our manners.

After we ate, we looked around the tiny apartment, smaller than our own, and observed meticulous care and planning. Fresh and clean, neat and pressed, table set, fire ready, flowers blooming. How lovingly Adrian had prepared this place for his bride.

"Will Anna ever see what Adrian has done to these rooms to please her?" Lillian asked. "Everything is so beautiful and sweet and thoughtful."

"Yes, it is. But we must hope and pray that there will be a 'happily ever after' here. I don't know Anna but if anyone deserves it, it's Adrian."

"Will there be a 'happily ever after' for us in our own home?"

"Yes, Lillian. We will return there safe and sound, soon I hope."

Lillian looked out the window. Through the curtains, she saw the highest tips of the inferno tickling the clouds, taunting them to rain. They refused.

Exhausted, she didn't dare fall asleep, concerned with where the unabated fire might travel next. Our place was somewhere between the fire and Adrian's and we were not there to water it down or protect it in any way. I read the worry lines on my wife's face and went over to the sofa, leaned down and kissed Lillian's forehead. Then did the same to little Lucy. I had no one to reassure me. Only my own feigned brave face.

"Don't be frightened," I said. "I won't let anything bad happen to us. Why don't you and Lucy get some rest? I'll stand watch."

After Lillian nursed our baby, she found an empty cabinet drawer in the kitchen, pulled it open, and placed Lucy there, wrapped in a thick blanket. Lillian tucked her own coat on top of our daughter to keep out the cold. She hugged me as if for the last time, pulled a crocheted throw over her weary body, and dozed for about a half hour before the noise of dynamiting jolted her awake.

"When will all this end?" she cried.

"I don't know," I said. "I just don't know."

Lillian and I tiptoed into the kitchen to check on little Lucy. As we looked over her, we hoped our family, and Adrian, and Anna would somehow find reprieve from what seemed like an endless fall from grace.

CHAPTER 14

ANNA

Sunday, 9:30pm

H.L. Mencken burst into the fifth-floor City Room of *The Herald* and barked orders at the growing number of journalists working within. The metal fireproof shutters had been closed on most of the building's many windows and doors, imprisoning everyone. Despite the resulting claustrophobia, and the dim lights blinking in trepidation, Mencken looked over his staff's shoulders, read their copy, made edits, and retreated to his small, glass-enclosed office.

I didn't know where to sit or what to do. I just stood there holding my pose like a person waiting to be photographed, while all around me flowed thoughts of passionate people, striving for perfection, their wastepaper baskets filled to overflowing, their rejected drafts thrown to the floor in angry rondures.

"Who are you and what are you doing here?"

"I'm Anna Bainbridge. I've been taking pictures of the fire for Mr. Mencken. He brought me here."

"I see. Lynn Meekins, Managing Editor. Where's H.L.?"

"He went in there," I said, pointing to his office.

Meekins addressed the thirty-some writers crowding the floor. Most were staff. Some were aspiring writers and some were experienced journalists who had been fired from *The Herald* and returned to help, in hopes of earning a second chance.

"Listen up! H.L. and I want this paper to be the best we've ever done. No sidebar stories, no fluff. Just fire. People all over the world will read your copy. Make it sing."

The percussive banging of typewriter keys composed copy. The tapping of nervous toes on the floor, and the passing of information from one reporter to another, like a song's memorable melody, filled the room.

One writer worked on a story about valiant efforts to save the German Zion Lutheran Church on Gay Street near Lexington. His headline read:

```
           Zion Church Afire

   Volunteer Firemen Ventured Upon Steep Roof

                To Save Building
```

I asked if I could take a peek at his copy. It read:

Flying sparks at 8:30pm. Roof slopes on both sides from the middle steeply. They had to straddle and crawl with buckets of water and managed to extinguish before fire trucks arrived.

I regretted seeing this story unfold on paper rather than in person and wished I could have climbed onto that roof myself to take pictures of firemen inching their way along the steep pitch. At the same time, I found all the activity in the City Room to be a beautiful symphony, each player contributing to the masterpiece.

It became obvious that the sweep of unfolding events had brought me to this moment. I allowed myself to dream of a future here and ponder how I might fit in as a real member of *The Herald* team. Before knowing it, I had flumped on an empty chair; the intoxicating thought of a career in journalism had made me swoon.

Joe Callahan, Mencken's assistant city editor, gave me a sharp look, then introduced himself.

"Why are you just sitting there? Get to work."

"I'm a photographer, not a writer. Mr. Mencken invited me. I'm his guest."

"What have you shot?"

Before I could answer him, Mencken's door flew open. The city editor stormed out of his office and yelled, "I've got the headline." He looked at one of the writers and said, "Connor, run this down to Printing straight away. Give it to Ryan and tell him I want it bold, two lines, no more."

It read:

HEART OF BALTIMORE WRECKED BY GREATEST FIRE IN CITY HISTORY

I couldn't believe that, not only was I in the middle of the fire, I was in the middle of the fire's story being told, pressed into print, actual proof of what was happening for those who lived through it to read, and all the generations that followed to study. I felt confident in my ability to succeed at *The Herald*, and become part of a group of reporters and photographers, admired for boldness and bravery, remembered for getting the perfect pictures, no matter the danger.

"Has anyone seen our photographers?" Mencken asked.

He had sent them to the fire hours before, and they should have been back by now. Not getting an answer, he rued their absence. It meant the paper would have to be type only, which often occurred. But in this case, pictures were imperative, if *The Herald* wanted to sell more copies than its competitors.

Discordant sounds of police whistles in the lobby below cut through the music in the room, already accompanied by the cadent tolling of the City Hall bell. Mencken sent one of his reporters to see what caused the disturbance.

"We have to get out. Our building's on fire," the man yelled when he returned.

"Impossible!" Mencken shouted, as if he possessed the power to reverse the circumstances.

Within minutes, Mencken, with his staff and me in tow, raced down the stairs, carrying galleys, page-proofs, pots of paste, pencils and the assignment book. We pushed through a wall of thick smoke, opened the massive front door, and made it to safety outside. Police officers bundled all of us across the street. The building housing *The Herald*, and several other businesses, would eventually surrender. Because of the closed shutters, it would take a while, several hours, to dash all hopes of saving the structure.

As it turned out, some of the windows had not been measured properly, so their shutters hadn't sealed tightly. Sly as it was, the fire took advantage of those mistakes to gain its foothold and write its own story.

H.L. directed, to no one in particular, "Fire and wood pulp make poor bedfellows. This is catastrophic!"

"I thought you said it couldn't burn," I retorted. "Now you not only don't have an office, you don't even have a paper."

Mencken's face reddened. I had intentionally insulted him, a slap to the face of a man offering me an opportunity that shouldn't have been diminished with snipes. Without responding, he walked a block away towards the owner of *The Herald*, whom he spotted with a group of fellow employees. I stayed put and watched the two men confer.

Mencken was ordered to continue covering the story as if nothing had changed. He quickly forgot about my nasty remark and carried on with his work right there in the street. I noted that Mencken's focus always stayed on task, come what may. He never lost sight of immediate priorities. I vowed to watch his every move and copy his ways. I would learn from someone confident in his decisions, even though he walked a high wire of his own.

By now, the building next to *The Herald's* was fully engulfed. H.L. wrote the story on the spot:

The flames leaped through it as if it had been made of matchwood and drenched with gasoline, and in half a minute they were roaring in the air at least five hundred feet.

Over the next half hour, Mencken and his staff worked the fire, while I followed, observing, noting and memorizing.

Against orders, Mencken returned briefly to his building to retrieve important materials. When he came out, Meekins, the managing editor, was waiting for him.

"What is the situation in there?"

"Most likely a cruel lost cause. Debris everywhere. Windows smashed. The air whistling fire through every crack and crevice. And, to think, just a little while ago we were at our posts, tapping out stories, designing the layout. Damnation!"

"Maybe the building can still be saved."

"I wouldn't bank on it."

"Listen, the boss has made arrangements for the *Washington Post* to print our fire edition tonight. He said to get your writers down there straight away. I'll go with you. We have to take a copyreader, some circulation men, and as many printers as possible. We should have enough material to publish the paper, even if it's only a few pages. But let's do it up as big as we can. Oh, one more thing. They won't do this free of charge. In exchange for printing the paper, they want the copyright on as many half-tones as we can supply. I hope you have some great pictures."

This news didn't sit well with Mencken at all. He appeared at a loss. His staff photographers and stringers should have returned to the office already in order to meet deadline. Since they couldn't gain access to the building, he didn't know where they might be, and he had no way to round them up quickly. I stood by, bearing the hint of a grin on my face, having learned nothing from my impertinence moments before.

"Well, it looks like you need me," I said.

"I don't need—"

"Okay, I'll just see if *The Sun* wants—"

"Wait. All right. Come with me to Washington. I don't even know if *The Post* can process film from a Brownie camera. Or make engravings in time for publication. For now, this is the best we can offer them. It will have to suffice."

Mencken didn't wait for my response. He presumed I would jump at the chance. He gathered his writers, who informed him that a charter train had just been secured for them at Camden Station.

"Everyone bound for Washington, gather around," he called.

"I can't go with you," I said.

"What? Why not?"

"Because my father and my fiancé—"

"You have a fiancé? If you're getting married, why are you looking for work? You should be thinking about home and hearth... motherhood, prams, baking biscuits."

"Wait a minute... I'll give you the rolls of film I've shot so far, but I want printed credit for any photographs published now or later, even if they're used for etchings or engravings. I'll stay here and continue to shoot pictures and gather information."

"You're making demands of me?"

"That's right. My work is worth something. And it looks like you don't have much of a choice at the moment. These pictures are going to sell your newspaper and you know it."

It didn't take Mencken more than a second to make up his mind.

"Very well. Have it your way. Give me the film."

I didn't reveal the real reason I hadn't agreed to go with Mencken. True, Washington was far away. And the story raged in Baltimore. But, deep down in my heart, I knew that going with Mencken to my honeymoon destination would seem like I was being unfaithful to Adrian.

I handed over the rolls of film, along with my log of frames. For some reason, I trusted Mencken. Or, perhaps, my motivation was more selfish than that. I wanted to see my name in print, credited with a photograph. I wanted to feel a part of something outside my own narrow world, and was willing to take the risk to make it happen, even giving those precious pictures to a virtual stranger, who might or might not make good on his word.

"The wind is shifting!"

"Everyone leave the area immediately!"

Shouts from firefighters on the next street grew closer. The wind had changed direction at will, pushing the fire away from City Hall and the Main Post Office, leaving both landmarks and the neighborhood east of the fire, where Adrian lived, unscathed. The gusts traveled west to east, then east to southwest, as if playing a children's game of tag.

As we moved away, the air filled with rumblings of a standoff at O'Neill's Department Store across from the Union Trust Building on Charles Street.

O'Neill's reputedly catered to an elite clientele, who expected personal service of the highest quality. The multi-story emporium carried the finest of everything, earning it the nickname, "The Store Of Specialty Shops."

"We will see what's going on there first," Mencken said to his staff. "We have time before the train leaves." Though uninvited, I went with them.

When we arrived, we found a crowd of police and firefighters facing Thomas O'Neill in the doorway of his building. On any other day, he would be standing there, dressed to the nines and smiling as he welcomed each of his customers by name. He wasn't smiling in this instance.

"You're not going to dynamite my store," he yelled.

Full of fire himself, Thomas O'Neill projected a towering presence, with flame red hair and a whisk broom mustache. The thirty-two-year-old Irish immigrant, born of potato famine survivors in County Caven, had inherited the invincibility of his forefathers.

"If you want to bring down this building, I will go with it. I am not moving."

Mencken beamed. "What high drama! Don't you agree?" he said. "And starring the perfect hero! Now this is a story."

He questioned bystanders and found out that when the fire had first gotten out of hand that morning, O'Neill drove to the Carmelite Convent on Biddle Street to pray with the nuns for God's mercy and guidance. When he left, he took holy water from their chapel to bless his store. After that, he increased the blessing. He stuffed cloth in all the spouts and air vents on top of his building, unplugged the water tower located there and let the contents pool. As a result, any roof-hopping flames were consumed, granting O'Neill's salvation from the fire.

I leaned in to Mencken.

"I'm going to shoot a picture," I whispered.

"I thought your camera only worked in daylight," Mencken said.

"Well, the flames down the street are brighter than daylight. I have to take the chance."

I didn't want to waste film but stepped forward anyway to capture the confrontation. When I pressed the shutter lever, it stuck.

"Damnation!" I cursed, the first oath I had ever sworn. Elizabeth would have been mortified, had she heard me say it. And Papa would have washed my mouth with Pears' Soap!

I thought for a second and reached up to the chatelaine pinned to my coat. I pulled the sewing needle out of its sheath and used it to nudge the lever loose. Praying for good luck, I snapped the picture. After turning the frame-winding key, I snapped another, in case the first shot hadn't taken.

Without realizing it, I was learning how to improvise, learning how to think fast on my feet, learning how to do my "job."

"Well, well, you have become quite the professional," Mencken mumbled under his breath. He wouldn't dare say it directly to me. Having good hearing, I put him on the spot, pouring salt on the wound.

"What was that? Speak up, Mr. Mencken."

All I got was a one-word reply, "Nothing."

Police and firefighters didn't try to forcibly remove O'Neill from his store. It was becoming obvious that the dynamiting strategy wasn't working as well as they had hoped. And they didn't want to get in trouble with one of Baltimore's most successful businessmen. They moved their operation away from O'Neill's, which didn't burn a cinder that night or throughout the fire's entire siege. When H.L. Mencken later interviewed Thomas O'Neill, the entrepreneur attributed the sparing of his business to divine intervention.

"Front page, below the fold," Mencken said to no one in particular.

"What does 'below the fold' mean?" I asked.

"You really don't know anything, do you? The newspaper is folded in half when you receive it, is that right?"

"Yes."

"Above the fold are the biggest or most interesting stories. Below the fold, where you would have to flip the paper to read them, are the lesser stories."

"I see. How do you decide...?"

H.L. must have had enough of me. Before I could finish the question, he and his staff had made for Camden Station, leaving me in their wake to fend for myself.

"My pictures will always be 'above the fold,' in case you are interested," I said to no one in particular.

CHAPTER 15

SAM

Sunday, 10:00pm

Adrian lumbered up behind Lillian. She was staring out the southwest window of Adrian's apartment while I listened to a passerby through the beveled glass pane.

"In Little Italy, they're soaking blankets in water and putting them on the gables of their houses to keep flames from leaping rooftop to rooftop, should the fire reach that far," the man said. "And the police have ordered everyone living there to sleep in their traveling clothes in case they have to evacuate quickly."

"Should we do the same?" I asked.

"That's what I'm going to do when I get home. Would, too, if I were you."

"Thanks for the information. Good luck to you, sir."

"The same to you and all of Baltimore," the man replied, as he hurried on his way.

I turned to my fretting wife. We would have to search through Adrian's belongings to find what was needed.

"What are you doing here?" Adrian asked.

"Oh, Adrian, you startled me. How are you feeling?" Lillian said.

"I'm better. I think the effects of the medicine have finally worn off. I'm a little more clearheaded."

"Good. How's the pain? Do you want more laudanum?"

"Not right now. The pain's not too bad. My knee mostly throbs and feels tight around the stitches. It's hard to walk, even with these crutches. What's going on? Why are you here? What day is it? What's happening with the fire? Have you heard any news of Anna?"

"Not so fast, Adrian," I said. "I'm sorry to say I've heard nothing of Anna. As for the fire, well, it just keeps spreading. We had to leave our home and we brought you here. Look through the curtains. See the tip of the Continental Trust Building on fire? It's really bad, Adrian."

"Why that building must be sixteen stories. On fire? All of it? Oh, no."

"I'm afraid even the tallest skyscraper in Baltimore can't stand up to the fire."

"I remember when it was built, just a couple of years ago. The architect, I think his name was Burnham... yes, Daniel Burnham, gave a grand interview to the newspapers. I'll never forget what he said: 'Make no little plans; they have no magic to stir men's blood and probably will not themselves be realized.' How he must feel now."

"Oh, Adrian, don't think of those things. It's all too unbearable," Lillian said.

"I'm sorry. I'll try not to. What time is it, Sam?"

"Around ten, ten-fifteen."

"Where's Anna? Where's my darling Anna?"

"I'm sure she's somewhere safe, Adrian," Lillian replied.

"I had a dream... I guess the medicine made my mind go crazy... I thought that Anna was... I can't bear to think about it. I thought she... that no one was around to help her, and she..."

"Don't worry about that now. It was just a nightmare. Nothing more," I said.

"Are you hungry?" Lillian asked. "You must be. There's some chocolate cake in the kitchen. I'm sorry to say, Sam and I already helped ourselves."

"That was for Anna when..." Adrian's voice trailed off.

Resignation showed in the tilt of his head as he hobbled towards the kitchen behind Lillian. She made Adrian a cup of tea and got him to eat some cheese and bread. He wouldn't touch the cake.

"Now that you're awake, Adrian, I think I'll venture out again and see what I can find," I said, entering the room. "Lillian, will you keep an eye on things here?"

"Oh, no, please don't go," Lillian cried. She feared for my safety and dreaded the responsibility of caring for Adrian alone. He'd already snuck out once.

"I must, dear, for Adrian. I'll be back soon, I promise."

"But what about soaking the roof?"

"That will have to wait, for now."

It took forty-five minutes to reach the eastern edge of downtown, where I was stunned to see how rapacious the fire had really become. The merchant district had already been obliterated. Now the financial district blazed against the dark of night. From this close, the Continental Trust Building took on the ritual guise of a Samhain torch.

When I reached Calvert & Baltimore Streets, the air felt solid and scorched. The rolling thunder of the fire was nearly deafening. A fireman warned me to stand back.

"Don't go any closer. The heat is pretty intense, must be twenty-five hundred degrees," he screamed at the top of his hot, tired lungs.

"Have you seen a young...?" I yelled.

"I can't help you. Get going."

Just blocks away, there was nothing but ruins. Most buildings were completely gone, while parts of others remained standing in charred determination, like dinosaur carrion.

The wind thrashed at about thirty-five miles an hour and I couldn't tell where it would push the flames next. I didn't know which way to turn. In no time, I became disoriented and fell victim to an attack of panic.

It seemed as if the ground beneath Baltimore had cracked and an eruption ensued, forcing the city grid to run with its sputum. Building after building, block after block, had been caught in its molten wake.

The fire didn't inch, but rushed towards The Basin, Baltimore's harbor area. And that's exactly where I was forced to go, no more confident in my abilities than I was the first time I'd ventured out.

At the docks, the stench of burning debris, dead fish, wharf trash, and rotting fruit filled my nostrils. The city reeked of evil and lust and omniscience. I stumbled over tobacco hogsheads, some lined up, others rolling around the street. The fire consumed a few of the barrels bound for Richmond or Lynchburg, Charlotte or Augusta. Smoldering tobacco leaves created a bitter extract, leaving anyone who dared to breathe it, including me, gasping for clean air.

Spasms of nausea gripped my stomach, threatening to boil up. I covered my nose and mouth with a handkerchief. Precious little oxygen penetrated the scrim, making me dizzy. I blinked rapidly, tears polluting the cloth. After blowing my nose hard, I wiped my eyes and trudged on.

Through the filthy fog, I could barely discern an outline of the oyster fleet in port, next to banana steamers, the tugs *Venus* and *Mary*, and revenue cutter *William Windom*. A lone fireboat, *The Cataract*, tried to maneuver between all the docked vessels in order to secure its best vantage point. Merchant ships, escaping to the Chesapeake Bay, collided in their haste and made it rough going for everyone.

Among local police and firefighters on the street, military sailors patrolled the harbor, and fire units from Philadelphia raced to head off the blaze before it hit Dugan's Wharf. Teamsters organized a hasty removal of shipping goods from the area. They used heavy equipment, as well as wheelbarrows, wagons, even hand baskets. To me it all seemed useless. Overcome, I wept.

Behind me the wind lifted kindling five whole blocks. It struck the Church of the Messiah on the corner of Fayette and Gay Streets, eventually leaving little more than the bell tower.

Sparks rained down on several other structures at the same time, like giant fingers reaching into a Victorian diorama to crush miniature beds, tables and pianos. The new fires changed the heading of the blaze east towards the Jones Falls and Little Italy. In an about-face, the wind pushed the flames back to Pratt Street near Charles.

By this time, firefighters from all points had converged and joined Baltimore's ranks... Frederick, Altoona, Harrisburg, York, Wilmington and New York. As if there weren't enough problems, units coming from the north by train had been delayed by an accident on the tracks.

In all, more than twelve-hundred firefighters now battled the blaze at the harbor and throughout the city.

The National Guard had arrived in full force to help bring about civil order. A member of the rank and file ordered me to vacate the area immediately.

"Please, I need to find someone, a young woman, petite, named Anna."

"You don't belong here. Go away, or I will see that you are arrested."

I was shocked. No one in authority had ever threatened me before. Never having served in war, I had not braved a situation so unthinkable. Frightened, I took off, running as fast as possible back towards Adrian's. I dodged debris flying in the wind, jumped hydrants, and slipped on the sidewalk's wet sludge.

The heat of the fire baked the air, turning it as thick as basalt. I couldn't breathe without feeling my lungs tighten. Sticky, fibrous fear glutted my stomach.

After several blocks, I hit an invisible wall. I panted wildly and my muscles tightened. My skin broke out in a cold sweat. It couldn't be helped... I leaned over and vomited violently into the gutter. An act so embarrassing and unbecoming a gentleman.

Fighting to regain my strength and composure, I looked up towards the sky.

I'm hallucinating.

Before me stood an impossible sight, one building, proud and resolute, slightly damaged but still standing among the detritus... the Alexander Brown & Sons investment firm, a structure dating back more than one hundred years.

Why had this building not been destroyed? Was it designed to withstand disaster? Were its owners sitting in God's favor? Maybe its sparing could be attributed to nothing more than a whim of the wind... or possibly destiny fulfilled.

I wrestled with my own ideology. The weft of my beliefs, twined throughout an unchallenged life, now began to show wear. What rhyme or reason had been placed in charge? So many questions that no one could answer rolled around in my head like the hogsheads on the street. Why was this fire happening?

What could the people of Baltimore have done to deserve this kind of vengeance? Certainly, a loving God would not have brought such horror upon us unprovoked. Would He? I became confused, and something happened I never thought possible... I doubted my faith. My desperation found its voice as I tightened my fists.

"Why? *Why?*" I screamed at the heavens.

The roar of the fire consumed my plea.

My head reeled with despair and, even more, with the feeling that God had abandoned Baltimore... and me.

With a deflated soul, I trundled back to Canton. When I got there, Lillian met me at the door. Tension flushed her pale, thin face and tears reddened her eyes.

"What happened? Is Lucy all right?" I asked.

"Yes, she's fine," Lillian murmured.

"Then what's the matter?"

"He's gone, Sam. Adrian's gone."

CHAPTER 16

H.L. MENCKEN

Sunday, 11:59pm

During the train ride to Washington, I composed O'Neill's story in longhand. When my staff and I disembarked thirty-five miles from the fire, I turned in the direction of Baltimore and the red bloom of fire on the horizon showed its magnitude.

"This must be the grandest and worst fire ever," I said.

Upon arrival at the *Washington Post* offices, I assumed my position as city editor for my own paper. I knew Scott C. Bone, Managing Editor of *The Post*, a good man and a fine journalist. But we tussled over information and copyrights, layout and headlines, until I realized my actions were counterproductive. This man was doing me a favor. Not the other way around.

Maybe I was just tired and still hung-over from that drinking soirée the night before. And hunger gnawed at my stomach, affecting my mood in a most unpleasant way. I pooled my staff's money, combining it with my own. A paltry $65 was all we had to live on for the next several days, covering lodging and food. The money wouldn't last long, especially if we enjoyed some liquid refreshments after pulling the edition to bed.

Through gritted teeth and arched eyebrows, I began to work in conjunction with the D.C. paper's staff. Jointly, we published thirty-thousand copies of a four-page fire edition that included this disclaimer.

The Herald to-day is printed by The Washington Post, whose courtesy to its contemporaries is proverbial.

All the Baltimore newspapers were burned out. The Herald building was the last to go, and there

were hopes almost until midnight that it would be saved. As it is, The Herald will be published daily by the best means it can command under the circumstances.

As impossible as it might seem, the newspaper made money on the fire edition by selling advertising space to owners of burned-out businesses, eager to inform their customers about temporary relocations. No one allowed the fire to be all-consuming, especially not the people who put everything into their work. I applauded those merchants for their tenacity in the face of disaster. Even before cleaning up, even without blueprints and new brick and mortar, Baltimore was rising from the ashes.

Sometime early Monday morning, maybe 4am or so, I snapped open the paper and felt its crispness, admired its neat columns standing at attention like the structures that once made up Baltimore's skyline. I breathed in its inky typeface and felt pleased, for the most part. Used to being in charge and unquestioned, I wasn't happy about this makeshift working arrangement. For the sake of *The Herald* and my own professional hide, I swallowed my pride and did what was best for all. With the perspective of hindsight, I would later write bluntly about the toll this experience took on me.

"When I came out of it at last I was settled and indeed almost a middle-aged man, spavined by responsibility and aching in every sinew, but I went into it a boy, and it was the hot gas of youth that kept me going."

I wasn't the only one fueled by a story beyond comprehension.

CHAPTER 17

ADRIAN

Midnight

"Where are you going?" I asked a neighbor, who was hitching his horse to a dray that had seen better days.

"I'm helping the fire department remove broken glass. Some of the main streets are blocked by debris and they can't get to the fire. There's good money in it."

"What route are you taking?"

"The fire's going strong down by The Basin. I have to go north above the fire and around the western edge."

"Can I ride along?"

"Thanks for the offer, Adrian, but you don't look like you'll be much help."

"I know. I need to find someone."

"It's pretty disorderly everywhere, Adrian. And it's already late. It won't be easy."

"Please, just get me close to Saratoga and McLane Place. I can find my way from there."

"At your own risk. You'll have to climb in the back."

Not much passed between us. I was nothing more than dead weight, useless cargo. I became lost in thoughts of Anna; fear circled my mind with each rotation of the wheels. After forty-five minutes, I gingerly stepped off the wagon several blocks from my destination, Anna's home. Continuing my journey on foot and crutch, I winced in newfound pain which reminded me that I wasn't as brave as I thought, and the bottle of laudanum remained at home.

Earlier that day, I had witnessed the fire raging near the Post Office. I had not seen the city's entrails exposed until this moment. Here, near where the fire started, it seemed as if I had been plucked from earth and set down on another planet, where everything was brown and black and smelled of fine ash that I breathed in but didn't exhale. The soot built up in my lungs until it felt like the ruins of the entire city lay inside me.

I could see, in the distance, the fury south near the harbor. The brightness of the flames there melanized my surroundings uptown.

It took me quite a while to make my way to Anna's neighborhood. I had to push aside a lot of rubble, and brush away the memory of that painful first meeting with Dr. Bainbridge, which seemed years ago now, although only a few months. I wanted nothing more than to find Anna at home, safe and sound. The wedding could wait. Confronting Anna's father could wait. I would interact with the doctor cordially, if found at home. I hoped Anna's father would reciprocate. Every effort had to go towards ensuring Anna's safety.

When I reached what I thought was Anna's block, it looked as black as the farthest reaches of a coalmine. The red brick row homes were shrouded in cloudy residue. The few remaining gas lamps on the street had been extinguished and there were no signs of electricity. It made finding Anna's address all the more taxing. I picked my way along, using my crutch like a blind man's cane. Even though I knew the street well, I still had to climb up steps here and there, feeling house numbers along the way.

Locating Anna's home, I knocked hard, knowing full well the consequences if I roused Anna's father from his sleep. I kept knocking.

After almost a minute, I saw through the window, a lit taper move towards the front door as if floating on air.

My heart leaped at the thought that Anna might be holding it. Just the same, I braced myself should her father open the latch instead. When the door opened, neither person faced me.

"Who are you? What do you want?" Elizabeth asked.

"Excuse me, ma'am, for calling at this late hour. I'm Adrian Crosby. I came to see Anna. Is she in?"

"What? Oh. Come in, quickly, before this flame blows out."

Elizabeth lit two wall sconces in the parlor and directed me to the settee. She paid no mind to my filthy pants. I was surprised to find that Elizabeth hadn't gone to bed yet. She was still dressed in uniform, as if expecting someone.

"I recognized you at the door. I remember the night you came here. That disastrous dinner," she said, shaking her head in recollection.

A hint of sympathy marked her inflection. Silence followed. Neither of us knew what to say. Elizabeth decided to speak first, curious to learn why I would be asking about my own bride.

"I know about your elopement with Anna. I'm Elizabeth, her nanny, if you didn't remember. Mr. Crosby, why have you come here asking about her? She's your wife. Isn't she with you?"

"No, ma'am, the wedding never took place."

"Never took place? Whatever on earth happened? Merciful heavens! Where might she be?"

"I have no idea. We were supposed to meet at St. Alphonsus to get married after the early Mass. I fell several blocks away and had to be taken to the hospital. I never saw her."

The gravity of this news hit Elizabeth like a suffocating gust of wind. Her hand flew to her face as if to prevent her head from falling. I tried to get up to offer comfort, without success. Falling back onto the seat, I could only offer her words, the same puppet sentences Sam and Lillian had used on me.

"I'm sure she's safe somewhere," I said. "Maybe she's with her father. He's not here, is he?"

"No, he left early this morning. I haven't heard from him today. As far as I know, he's still at the hospital."

We sat in silence for a while. It was then that Elizabeth noticed my blood-stained trousers and understood its presage.

A feeling of dread entered the room like slinking smoke. A draft of air caused the lamps to flicker. One blew out. Elizabeth gasped. I shuddered. We heard a slow creak. The front door had opened.

I jumped up in anticipation, glad for the support of crutches this time.

The tall silhouette of a man stood in the hallway outside the parlor. He stepped into the room, where light from the single burning lamp gave his ears a translucent, red-orange glow and pitched his face in doleful shadow. He looked as if some sort of inner seething had started to bubble up to the surface, ready to explode.

"Who is here?" the voice said.

"Doctor Bainbridge!" Elizabeth cried, her eyes darting from her employer to me.

When the doctor spotted me, he stepped closer, then stopped in restraint. His eyes darkened and both eyebrows shrank in anger. It seemed that I drew out some pent-up emotion that Dr. Bainbridge had been storing for ages.

"So, you two were together all along. You lied to me. Get out of my house this instant. Elizabeth, fetch Anna. I want to speak to her."

"Doctor Bainbridge, you have the wrong impression," Adrian interjected. "I came here tonight in search of Anna. I haven't seen her in two days."

"I don't believe you. Elizabeth, do as I say."

"But, sir, Mr. Crosby is telling the truth. I haven't seen Miss Anna myself today."

"What? Then where is she?"

"That's what we're trying to determine," the housekeeper said.

"Elizabeth, go find a constable. Elizabeth, now!"

"Yes, sir."

Elizabeth grabbed her shawl and ran out into the night, leaving me alone with Anna's father. The air between us hung heavy and caustic. Our eye contact, predator to prey.

"You know more than you are saying. It will be to your benefit to tell me everything before the officer gets here," Dr. Bainbridge said.

"Anna and I were supposed to meet at church this morning."

I purposely left out any mention of elopement, even though I felt no shame or regret. I might have told Anna's father the whole truth if it would have been productive. For my bride's sake, and to clear the path that would lead to her, I chose my words with utmost care.

"So, you are still seeing each other, against my wishes?"

"Yes, sir. But that's not important now. We must find Anna."

"Not important! She would be home safe in her bed this very minute if she hadn't made an appointment to meet you. This is all your fault."

"Doctor Bainbridge, your daughter and I never met at church. The fire started and I fell and hurt my leg, and... well... I have a friend looking for her. Do you have any idea where she might be?"

"I heard..." he said, abruptly stopping.

He refused to confide in me anything he knew, even for his daughter's sake. His desire was to punish me.

"...no, I do not know where Anna might be," Dr. Bainbridge replied.

Elizabeth returned with a patrolman at her heels.

"What's going on here?" the officer asked.

"My young daughter is missing, and this man knows where she is. He won't tell me."

"You are mistaken, sir," Elizabeth said.

"What do you know of this? Are you hiding something from me, too? If you are, your position here is in grave danger, regardless of your years of service."

Elizabeth and I eyed each other in quiet complicity. Neither dared betray the implied trust in the other. We could match the doctor's surreptitious behavior tit for tat.

"I will contend with you later," Dr. Bainbridge warned his housekeeper. "Officer, take this man out of my home immediately. I can't stand the sight of him."

"Do you want to press charges, sir?"

"Yes, kidnapping! Just... just take him to the precinct and I will come later, after I've eaten and slept."

"Yes, sir. We will hold him at The Northern."

I offered no protest, not wanting to make a bad situation worse. I thought I'd give Dr. Bainbridge cooling-off time, and hoped Elizabeth would find a way to placate Anna's father.

Later, at Northern District police station, several miles away in Hampden, I stood behind bars in a holding cell with looters and money thieves and other people who had taken advantage of tragedy for personal gain. I tried to carve out a small space to stay away from them. I wondered how long I would be left in a place so cold and hard and inhumane, that offered little privacy, that stank from curved urine drains lining the floor, that was overrun with mice and littered with their droppings.

Evil stares bore through the dank jail. I knew that if Anna's father pressed charges, I might be there quite a while. The surroundings arrested all hope. As long as I sat locked away, I wouldn't be able to help search for my beloved Anna.

"What are you doin' here? You don't look like none of us," a cellmate said.

I glanced down at my Sunday best and realized I was too well dressed for this brood. Startled, I didn't know how to respond. Maybe this stranger was taunting me into some kind of physical altercation or, thinking I had money... theft.

"Hey, I'm talkin' to you. Answer me."

Too weak and despondent to fight, I chose to unburden myself. If I appeased this man, he might leave me alone. So I told him the truth, the entire story in every detail, naming names, and when I finished, the man simply walked to the other side of the cell without saying a single word. He never even introduced himself.

I felt as plundered as the city. I had to rest. Sitting on the cleanest part of the floor, I leaned back against the wall, and sighed as though releasing the last black breath of life left inside me.

CHAPTER 18

ELIZABETH

1am

After Adrian and the constable left, I removed myself from the doctor's castigation. I went into the kitchen to prepare a plate of cold meat, fruit and bread for him. Maybe all he needed was food to settle his sour mood. For what other reason would he have spoken to me so disrespectfully? After all my years of devoted service, had I deserved to be keelhauled?

Maybe he was justified, and I should be chastised for not speaking up sooner. Anna might be safe at home, had I been loyal to my employer and reported my charge's clandestine plans when I learned of them weeks before. But I felt my first duty was to Anna, not her father. And, even though my situation and wage depended on Dr. Bainbridge, my assignment had been his daughter's welfare. But she was an adult now and could marry whomever she pleased. The fire had simply gotten in the way, like a muddy rut preventing a carriage from reaching its destination.

"Open a bottle of sherry," the doctor said, entering the room.

I automatically reached for the corkscrew on my chatelaine. Only pinholes of the phantom brooch remained in my apron. Pressing my hand on my chest, I hoped Anna's wedding gift and letter had brought comfort to the bride-to-be, now jilted by terrible circumstance, now all alone somewhere with no husband to reach out to in the night.

"Sir, I've misplaced the corkscrew."

"Never mind, then. I need food more than anything."

Dr. Bainbridge took the plate upstairs to his bedroom suite and closed the door. I retired to my own room next to the kitchen and collapsed in a quake of tears, so filled with mixed emotions that had no other escape.

Sleep did not find me. I doubted it found the doctor, either. All of Baltimore must have been suffering from the kind of insomnia that even the most beautiful of dreams would fail to assuage.

CHAPTER 19

ANNA

Monday, 3:00am

Mencken had been gone for quite some time, leaving me misplaced, out of step. My mood shifted like the capricious wind. My stomach growled, body ached and my swollen feet begged for soothing. My soul felt as aphotic as the inside of my Brownie, as lifeless as unexposed film.

All around me stood burned out shells, buildings that once teemed with activity and now sat vacant. I saw them for what they were, nothing but façades, fronts with no substantive backing. Frauds. Like me. I was no photojournalist; I was just a dilettante with a Brownie camera taking pictures. When I turned Mencken down, aspirations of becoming anything more had evaporated.

He had just been humoring me all along. More likely, lacking any other alternative, he used me. I didn't have what it takes to live this lifestyle. I didn't even have the courage to go with Mencken to Washington on the spur of the moment. And, how senseless of me... I hadn't arranged a way to deliver more pictures to him.

My energy was doused with the realization that I was, in fact, worthless, as bare as the building beams standing next to me and as bone-weary.

I longed for my canopied featherbed but I couldn't return to my father's home, which I could no longer claim as my own. I didn't know where to go, so I slowly walked south towards the fire. That was home now.

I moved through the blackened wake of the blaze north of the fire. Nothing worth photographing existed. No shapes to form in the fixer. The negatives would show no contrast between light and dark because everything through the viewfinder was rife with Cimmerian scree. One giant black hole. I thought it might absorb me. And there would be no evidence, not even a photograph, to prove that Anna Bainbridge had been here.

To shake the gloom, I raced the rest of the way. Flames had advanced across Lombard and now threatened Pratt Street, which ran along the piers at The Basin. Unbeknownst to me at the time, firebrands had started a second fire northeast of the harbor on, ironically, Water Street. In a matter of hours, the two fires would reach out to one another, lock arms, and create a chokehold on the wharf area.

Somehow, I found the strength to continue taking pictures. It was the only thing to do. I didn't know why, but the flames seemed to fuel me. As oxygen feeds a fire, fire fed me.

I had to conserve film, though. Half of my rolls had already been shot. And many pictures might not have taken, given my inexperience and the fixed aperture setting in the camera. Still, I vowed to go on.

And since Mencken and his staff now resided in Washington, I needed to spend more time gathering information. But what to write on? My log had gone with Mencken. I heaved a deep sigh, knowing there was no choice in what to use. I pulled the Carrollton menu from my pocket, turned it over, disallowing any emotion to enter my decision, and started noting observations. To conserve paper, I used few words, even creating my own style of shorthand in the tiniest script possible.

```
Out of contl... ships threatnd... hdrds of
ffiters... mass confu... natl gd... unload
ships... 1 fboat... unbear heat... blk smoke...
terfying
```

My spirit rose above the smoke clouds; I had become useful again. The fire in my belly reignited, though it wouldn't last long.

For a better view of the panorama, I took a wide berth around the fire at the docks and headed towards Federal Hill. On the way, I spotted a crate of bananas and, without a single thought, took two, one for now and another for later. Such a small gesture, innocuous to most, but so wrong in my overbearing conscience.

Always do the right thing, Anna, especially when no one is watching.

I could see my father behind me in that mirror, tapping my shoulder.

I know, Papa, but I'm hungry. And the whole world has gone mad, I thought. *Can't I, just this once, step over your strict line between right and wrong?*

Guilt followed me all the way to the foot of Federal Hill. I had conspired against my father. Run away from home. Lied to a police officer. Cursed. Now I stole. What was wrong with me? Had I slipped off that high wire and fallen through the safety net my former life had provided? My first transgression, planning to elope, had led me down a dark, steep slope. How far would I tumble?

My actions had been so out of character, yet they served a noble purpose. Didn't they? Didn't the end justify the means?

I was too hungry to grapple with my thoughts. As I climbed the hill, I took my mind off my troubles by peeling the first banana and enjoying every bite defiantly. For good measure, I ate the second. By the time I reached the hilltop, the inner struggle had worked its way free.

Federal Hill, a looming mound of earth on the opposite side of the harbor from the fire, was named in honor of Maryland's ratification of the Constitution and its celebration. It overlooked all of downtown Baltimore. The inaugural festivities held there had included spectacular fireworks and massive bonfires. Now the landmark stood poised in the path of an unhappy blaze running rampant in its own morbid celebration.

The scene before me was frightening. The fire had become ineffable. It burned like condemnation. The air roiled with heat. I could barely breathe. Still, I raised my Brownie and got back to work, shooting the fiery skyline in fractions. But the confines of each frame couldn't possibly convey the whole story. The panoramic transmogrification could no more be captured on a negative than two fingers could reach up and snuff out the sun. I stopped shooting and stood there among all other onlookers, transfixed in awe by the sheer magnitude of loss.

Fireballs burst free from the blaze and plumed into the sky. Horrifying to me, indeed. At the same time, as contradictory as it might seem, I felt respect for the fire's power and purpose. Closing my eyes, I resolved to be that determined.

When I looked farther north, near home, I saw nothing but blackness, as if the world were really flat and the drop into oblivion lay just beyond the fire.

I worried about my loved ones. Doubts crept in once again, challenging my decision to photograph the blaze. How long had I gone without thought for anyone's well-being but my own? How uncaring I had been. I wondered if anyone had been looking for me all this time. Whom had I put in danger with my lapse in judgment?

You're a reckless, selfish girl. You deserve whatever happens to you now. You could lose Papa's love and Adrian's devotion, I thought.

I had gambled all or nothing and clearly lost. What was left of my life resembled the vast, once familiar landscape degenerating right in front of me.

I had to find out if there were any sparks left in the ashes. I decided to go home, back to Saratoga Street to Papa and Elizabeth, if they were still there. After what I had put them through these last nineteen hours, each seemingly as long as a year of my life, I knew I had to face them and take my lumps. I hoped they would understand. Maybe Adrian would, too. The biggest problem eating away at me was... I had no idea what to say to any of them. How could I possibly justify my actions?

I ran down Federal Hill and around the docks on Light Street, heading up Liberty. Everywhere, officials redirected me until somehow, in all the chaos, I ended up on St. Paul, a few blocks from Water Street. I tried to turn north towards home but, in a flash, the Water Street fire grew and blocked my way. The McCormick Spice building and The Maryland Institute College of Art were raging, burning to the ground. I turned west and tried to go up Charles Street. Abandoned emergency vehicles and streetcars, vermilion with fire, formed a phalanx. I traveled east, thinking I could access Calvert Street. No matter where I moved, flames surrounded me, closing in. I lacked direction.

Panicking, I ran down narrow unnamed streets and desolate alleyways. Before I knew it, all escape routes were consumed by flames.

I was trapped. Between two fires.

It seemed my life had become wedged between two fires, one a desire to become Adrian's wife, and the other a passion to become a photojournalist.

I knew Papa would step in and extinguish both.

My strength diminished, I backed up against a wall for support. There was no way out. Not a soul was near. It became entirely up to me to free myself from impending death.

Instead of feeling like time was running out, time became all I had. My mind rewound and wandered back years, when I was a child of eight.

"Please, Papa? Tell me what happened to Mama."

I had been a toddler when Mama passed away and yearned to know her, anything about her, especially why she left Papa and me so long ago.

To a child so young, death defined a scary place that had no doors or windows or any way out. A precocious girl, I needed the comfort of knowing.

"Not today, Anna."

"Yes, Papa, today."

Papa's face contorted into that same pained expression he wore whenever I pried into Mama's passing. He resented repeated requests to delve into the very part of his past he wanted to forget.

"Anna, we've gone over this before. She died of scarlet fever during the epidemic."

"I know that, Papa, but what really happened when she died? Where did she go?"

He thought for a while. He had seen many patients die. Where their spirits went, who could say? How could he tell me something he didn't know himself? God. Heaven. Hell.

Purgatory. These were all metaphysical. His world was tactile... muscles and bones and veins.

At the time, I didn't know he was hiding behind self-recrimination. But he had to appease me in some way. He knew I would just keep asking.

When he finally spoke, I was moved by his tenderness. I had no way of knowing that his words were self-serving, and he didn't even believe some of them.

"Look up, Anna. What do you see?"

"I see blue sky and lots of fluffy, white clouds."

"What do you think of when you see pretty clouds?"

"Angels."

"Well, your mother was a good person in every way, Anna. She rarely focused on herself, only others. I thought of her as my angel."

"Tell me more, Papa."

"On the day Mama died, a small, fluffy white cloud floated down from the sky and landed on your mother's shoulders like the first, sweet snowflake of winter. The cloud swirled and curved and coiled until two arcs rose from the mist, luminous and pure white, and feathers formed and fluttered in the cool afternoon breeze. She had wings, Anna. And not just any wings. Your mother's wings broadened beyond the span of the greatest trumpeter swan. And their flurry made the air smell like the vanilla pound cake she used to bake for Sunday socials. Mama's wings billowed and paused, billowed and paused, until she looked down and saw that her feet no longer touched this earth. She smiled serenely. Then, like the soft, gentle shift of those clouds in the sky right now, she billowed all the way up to heaven. Oh, Anna, Mama's fine now. There's no need to fret for her. She's very happy where she is. Now, I'm getting hungry. Let's go inside and have Elizabeth fix us some cinnamon bread and a nice cup of tea."

I had never seen Papa so sweet and generous before. I had fallen under the false impression that he truly gave of himself, for once. I stood up slowly, not wanting this precious moment to end. As we turned towards the house, Papa rested his hand on the nape of my neck, right between the shoulder blades, a rare show of affection that I misread completely.

"Papa, I feel something on my back. Am I growing wings, too? Am I about to die?"

"No, child. Ahead of you are many clear, blue skies."

At that moment, I knew I would not die in the fire. If my father couldn't help me, if Adrian couldn't help me, if I couldn't even help myself, Mama would. I closed my eyes and prayed out loud.

"Mama, help me. Please save me from dying this way. I'm not ready. I need to make peace with Papa before I go. I need to see Adrian once more, to explain. My own selfishness led me here, I know. I shouldn't be so obstinate. I should be more thoughtful, more loving. I should be more like you. Help me, Mama. Help me."

A strong gust of wind swirled and pushed me as if I had no control over where I was going. It turned me like a mother readying her child to play a game of pin-the-tail-on-the-donkey. The blindfold that had kept me from finding my way came undone and I could clearly see a narrow breezeway between two row houses. Its arch sat so low that even I had to bend down to enter. I didn't know if I would find safe haven on the other side but I trusted my mother's guidance.

My direction became clear.

I crouched and ran, feeling every brick inside the tunnel, counting off five, ten, fifteen, twenty feet to freedom.

On the other side, I gasped for air and, much to my surprise, felt oxygen lift my lungs. Exhausted, I bent over and breathed and breathed and breathed. After a minute or so, I stood up straight, inhaling normally.

Looking into the distant sky over my neighborhood, my eyes befell a patch of black night contrasted by a hint of nimbus that circled and glowed like a halo. For the first time in hours, I smiled. And, for the first time in my life, I felt Mama's love.

I faced the darkness of home, then turned and faced the light of the fire. Where to go? I didn't have to choose. The decision was made for me. The hands of my mother rested on the nape of my neck. And the push that sent me to photograph the fire in the first place returned me there.

CHAPTER 20

DR. BAINBRIDGE

Monday, 7:00am

I sat up in bed with a start, as though I had forgotten something. Or maybe it was a feeling of foreboding. I couldn't tell. It seemed as if something hewing and toothy were gnawing at my soul, leaving a moldy residue that couldn't be fettled with a scalpel.

A conflicting image of Victoria appeared in my mind. She smiled with her arms around Anna, not as a little girl, but as the young woman she had grown to be. I didn't want to dwell on what it meant. The thought was inconceivable. There still had to be time... time for Anna to beg my forgiveness.

I chased away the presentiment by handling a more practical matter, getting dressed. Not wanting to face my own image in the mirror, I hurried without performing any morning ablutions.

Even if I had used a razor and brush, I wouldn't have recognized the man staring back at me. For some reason, I felt like I had been turned inside out, seemingly overnight, and an autopsy of my life had already ensued. I didn't want to see the results.

Downstairs, Elizabeth stirred in the kitchen. She squeezed fresh orange juice to pair with a simple breakfast of cold sausages. She must have still been on edge from what had transpired the night before because she jumped when I entered the doorway.

"Oh... good morning, sir," she said. "Here is your breakfast. I'm sure you're very hungry."

"This is not what I want."

"I'm sorry it's so meager, Doctor. I had no way to cook something heartier, what with the..."

"I'm not referring to food. I want information. My breakfast will go down much easier if you tell me what you know about Anna and that man."

"Oh please, sir, don't press the issue. I have only Anna's best interest at heart. She's like a daughter to me."

"Don't say something so blasphemous. You know how I felt about Victoria, how I still feel."

"I'm sorry, sir. But I love Miss Anna so much."

"Tell me what you know."

"Please, Doctor Bainbridge."

"Tell me, or I'll call another constable and you will suffer the same fate as that man who tried to steal my daughter from me."

In all the years Elizabeth worked for me, she had never seen me so loose with my emotions... except when Victoria died. Elizabeth probably couldn't fathom why I was acting so strangely. I didn't even know myself.

"Well, sir, Anna and Adrian planned to be married yesterday morning at St. Alphonsus. They never met, because of the fire."

"They conspired to elope? And you knew about this? Did you help arrange this misalliance?"

"No, Doctor Bainbridge. I learned of the wedding just recently. While cleaning, I found a note revealing their plans among Anna's things. I didn't tell her of my discovery."

"You should have told me."

"Anna is of legal age, sir. She can make up her own mind. She knew you disapproved of Mr. Crosby. And, I guess, she felt she had no choice."

"How dare you reproach me!"

"I love Miss Anna, sir. I would risk anything for her happiness, even addressing you this frankly, even losing my situation."

"*Love.* What do you know of it? You never married. You never bore children."

"I know that if I had been blessed with a little girl of my own, I would have dedicated my life to her upbringing and happiness. That is what I tried to do with Miss Anna. But you always fought me whenever I got too close."

"You weren't her mother."

"She needed a feminine hand. She needed me."

"She didn't need you. She needed..."

My voice trailed to a whisper. I was defeated.

"...me. She needed me. And I... I wasn't always there."

I knew that one day my past would find me hiding under a blanket of regret. I realized how badly I had neglected my daughter, just as I had neglected Victoria when she needed me most. I rubbed my forehead as if to erase the blame.

Hanging my head, I let out a recreant sob, which I quickly masked by clearing my throat, and spoke as if Elizabeth weren't in the room.

"Anna, Anna, Anna, I wanted so much more for you than what I was willing to give."

"That's the point, Doctor Bainbridge. She found so much more... in Adrian."

I nodded, no longer possessing the energy to scold Elizabeth for speaking out of turn. Every word she had said hit its target. Covering my eyes with my hands, I silently begged forgiveness.

Elizabeth didn't speak against me again. She simply walked over to the table and put the plate and a glass of juice down in front of me.

"Please, sir, eat something. It will give you strength."

I picked up the napkin as Elizabeth went back to her quarters. After forcing down breakfast, I retreated to my study, eased into my leather wing chair and propped my legs on the ottoman. I had always found peace there among my textbooks and medical journals. Now, the surroundings brought me no comfort. I felt disoriented, as if the chapters I knew by heart had discomposed on the pages.

I decided that, as soon as I could collect myself, I would return to the hospital. I had to. I was needed there. At least, that's what I still said to myself. Truth be told, I wanted to escape, as always. The hospital served as my sanctuary, where an empty heart and family obligations were forbidden entry. I would stay occupied with continuous emergencies, the greater good, as I liked to think of it.

The gnawing stepped up its efforts.

Opening the desk drawer, I carefully pulled out a small photograph of Victoria set in an oval frame. I had once kept it on the desk but found my wife's face a constant reminder of how I had failed her. And I didn't want to risk Anna finding it.

"Victoria, I am lost. What should I do? Help me, my love," I sighed.

Closing my eyes, I sat in silence and took controlled, even breaths. After a while, something stirred in me. It was the vibration of an inner re-alignment. My soul warmed ever so slightly and opened just a crack. I had not felt this way since Victoria lived. The sensation grew powerful and sweet. It began to thaw my cold resolve.

The thin, amorphous veil of perfection fluttered. The soft focus shifted and, for a second, I glimpsed a defined image. The image of a father.

I started to feel paternal. These feelings were pure and unconditional, not prejudiced by bitterness and disappointment. I wanted so badly to fight them. It was easier to live in the comfort of mistakes than the discomfort of change.

Elizabeth stood in the doorway with her few possessions packed in two bags. With nothing to say, she started for the front door, carrying a lifetime of memories, mostly happy because of Anna. Her most prized possessions I was forcing her to leave behind... dignity, loyalty, usefulness.

"Where are you going?" I asked.

"Sir, given the circumstances, I can hardly expect to remain in your employ."

"Elizabeth, I... I need you. I need you to be here in case Anna comes home while I'm gone."

"Are you going back to the hospital, Doctor Bainbridge?"

"No, I'm going in search of my daughter."

A smile broadened on Elizabeth's face. She put down her things and took off her coat and hat.

"Yes, sir. I will stay right here. Yes, sir."

I didn't appreciate Elizabeth's barrage of approval. I donned my coat and wrapped a scarf around my neck without so much as a "Thank you" or "Good day." The thought escaped me that I hadn't bathed, shaved, or brushed my hair. I left in such a hurry that only the sound of the slamming door proved my exit.

Where to start? Do I know so little about my own daughter that I can't figure out where she might be, and with whom? Could Anna still be taking pictures of the fire? That's the last place I want to go.

Not that facing danger frightened me. I was trying to talk myself out of facing Anna. So I paid a neighborhood errand boy to get word to the hospital that I had a family emergency and didn't know when I might return there. The hospital had to understand, especially since I had put in such long hours the day before. My absence must have come as an anomaly to them, being the first time I ever put family before work.

Flagging a newspaper hawker, I bought a copy of *The Herald,* then walked several blocks north, where a barouche for hire picked me up and carried me away in the opposite direction. I thought I'd handle some unfinished business first, in Hampden, at the Northern District police station.

CHAPTER 21

SAM

Monday, 7:00am

The plangent assault of a ship's horn, announcing the arrival of a German immigrant liner at Locust Point near Fort McHenry, crossed The Basin and reached as far as Canton.

It woke me. Tiptoeing out of bed without disturbing my wife, I peeked through the curtains and saw, much to my horror, what appeared to be sparks dancing luridly right outside the window. My heart stopped beating for a split second. I blinked, wiped the sleep from my eyes, and looked again. This time, I saw speckles of dawn's first light glistening on dewy tufts of grass and shiny cobblestones, and glass windowpanes across the street.

A sigh of relief made Lillian stir.

"Sam?"

"Oh, I didn't mean to wake you, dear. Please go back to sleep."

"I'll see about breakfast. You drifted off without eating last night. You have to be famished."

"I must admit, I am."

"How about using the washstand first?

I glimpsed in the mirror. If I hadn't known better, I would have sworn I faced someone else. I resembled a man who had just cleaned a chimney. Fine lampblack clung to my blond hair and fair skin. The sooty smears of a master sweep wrinkled my hands. I hoped I had not soiled Adrian's bed linens but knew without looking that I must have. So ill and exhausted the previous night, I fell asleep in my clothes. A quick glance at the bedding revealed the evidence.

"Oh, no," I said.

"I'll wash the sheets in the tub, Sam. I feel terrible that we slept here. This should have been Adrian's wedding bed."

"I feel bad, too. By any chance, did Adrian come home last night?"

"No, Sam."

"I'm concerned."

"Sam, I know what you're thinking. I don't want you going out again, especially after what you suffered last night."

Having seen the fire and its aftermath up close already, I didn't want to leave any more than Lillian wanted me to. It didn't beckon me again. But I worried for Adrian, concerned about how long his leg would hold out and how long he could go without medication. Maneuvering anywhere near the fire was treacherous enough. It would be doubly difficult for a man on crutches. Would Adrian be able to move out of harm's way fast enough?

"Are you comfortable staying here with Lucy?"

"Oh, Sam, no."

"Lillian, I have to search for Adrian. The fire has moved away from this area. You have food and shelter here. You should be fine."

"What if the fire comes back? What if Lucy and I have to leave? Where will we go? How will I find you? No, I'm not comfortable staying here. This isn't our home. I can't continue eating Adrian's food and sleeping in his bed. If you remember, we were not invited. We just came."

"Dear, I think, given the circumstances, Adrian would understand."

"Can't we just go back to our place?"

"What if Adrian returns? Who will be here to help him and dose his medicine?"

"And what if he returns with Anna? What if they got married and want to be alone?"

"They could not have gotten married during all this mayhem. Please, Lillian, I don't want to argue. We have never fought."

I stroked Lillian's raven black hair and curled her chin into my hand. My eyes pleaded with her.

"I will do as you wish," she said. "But, Sam, you must be careful yourself. I want you to come back, too."

"Don't worry, I will."

I washed up and ate a quick breakfast, checked on Lucy, who was napping again, kissed my wife and, without showing any sign of trepidation, closed the door behind me to take on the day.

Drops of melting ice fell from trees like tears, one after another lamenting the loss of a whole city at the hands of a heartless, fallen star still burning brightly at The Basin, and still smoldering throughout downtown Baltimore.

I didn't want to go there unless totally necessary. And I had no idea where Adrian might have gone. To the fire? To Anna's home? To the church? I stood on the sidewalk in front of Adrian's apartment and tried to divine a plan.

"You look lost."

"Well, you could say that. Actually, I'm looking for someone who might be lost."

"Oh? Who is that?"

"His name is Adrian."

"Adrian? Adrian Crosby?"

"Yes, do you know him?"

"Certainly. I gave him a ride last night."

"Where did you take him?"

"Oh, ah, let me think. He asked me to stop at, ah, McLane Place, and maybe..."

"Saratoga? Was it Saratoga Street?"

"Might be. No, somewhere south of there, I think. I really don't remember. I'm sorry. Docs that help you at all?"

"Yes, it does. Thank you, sir."

Relief energized me. I was glad that Adrian had not put himself in danger and, instead, had gone to the church, or perhaps Anna's house.

I knew it was a long walk. But I felt no compulsion to hurry this time. I figured Adrian must be safe, wherever he was. Pulling up the collar of my coat, I set off for St. Alphonsus. If I didn't find Adrian there, I planned to try the Bainbridge residence again. I had no idea how I'd be received. From what Adrian had told me,

Anna's father would most likely be as stern as the fire. For now, Dr. Bainbridge emerged as the lesser of two evils.

At church, people gathered for Mass, while the priest donned his vestments in the sacristy. Scanning the crowd, I couldn't find a single person who fit Anna's description. No sign of Adrian either. I stood in the vestibule until all the worshippers had assembled. Assured that Anna and Adrian weren't among them, I headed west towards Anna's home.

No one answered when I called. I gathered my thoughts and realized I'd have to locate Dr. Bainbridge. Anna's father had to know something by now. Would he tell me—a stranger—what he knew about his daughter's whereabouts, especially when the intent was to ease Adrian's mind?

The hospital sat a fair distance away and the wind still whipped. Trolleys weren't working and, even though hansom cabs were picking up fares nearby, I didn't have the money to pay for one. Only my legs would carry me where I wanted to go, and they had been greatly overworked already.

I walked and walked and walked. By now, it must have been mid-morning. When I reached the hospital, dozens of people awaited treatment. They looked stunned as well as hurt.

"Excuse me. Excuse me, please. I'm looking for Dr. Bainbridge. Can you direct me to him?"

I interrupted medical staff and asked this question several times. Most people just shook their heads; some didn't respond at all, too busy with emergencies. Finally, a nurse said the doctor would probably not arrive any time soon, news that dismayed me greatly.

Outside the hospital, I wished a streetcar would come by. A ride back to Adrian's apartment would have been most welcome. Unbeknownst to me, the Power Plant annex, recently built on the southeast edge of the Pratt Street piers, had been damaged enough by the fire to shut down the electrical system that operated the trolleys and streetlights, even though the main structure itself, with its four tall smokestacks, remained unwavering against the flames.

I didn't know how to get home. The faith and hope that had fueled me this far were all but exhausted. Not the type of man to beg a favor of someone else, particularly a stranger, I had no choice. I stopped a man at the reins of a horse-drawn wagon and asked him for a ride.

"I'd be glad to accommodate you, but I'm not heading to Canton. I'm carting coal to the steam-powered fire engines."

I took this as a sign that I had to go back to the heart of the blaze one last time.

"May I go with you?"

"Of course. I could use the company."

Twenty minutes later, I stepped down from the wagon on the west end of Pratt Street. The fire still raged. I cast a gaze over the entire scene. My focus was drawn to individual people, mostly firefighters, and men with badges and weapons.

Then, an aberration caught my eye. A petite woman. Her clothes looked like they had once been fine. Now they resembled charity castoffs worn by a person without a home.

What's that in her hand, a small box? No, it's a camera.

"Anna, Anna Bainbridge!" I called out over the cacophony.

The petite woman stopped and squinted as if trying to figure out my identity. Turning on her heels, she ran away in the direction of the fire, looking like a wild animal eluding a predator.

"Anna, wait! I'm a friend of Adrian," I yelled, running after her.

Anna moved as fast as a cat. Before I knew it, she had escaped into the tangled jungle of people, emergency equipment and wreckage.

I didn't want to go after her. The scene frightened me. The blaze still ate away at the harbor and it seemed like firefighters had multiplied tenfold. There were hundreds of them, pulling hoses in every direction. Anna maneuvered through the area with ease. For me, it was nearly impossible. I didn't despair. After all, I had good news. I decided to head north and search for Adrian again to tell him what I knew to be true.

Anna was alive!

Catching a ride with a man clearing debris, I reached Anna's doorstep in half an hour, wondering if Adrian had found his way there by now. He had not.

This time, I smiled in relief as my knock was answered, entrance was gained, and a chair and refreshments were provided. I had seen Anna. Now, I sat in her home with someone she knew, Elizabeth, who was glad to see me and welcomed my news with a grateful heart.

I gave thanks, too, for these tiny steps forward in my search and the comforts of this grand home, resplendent in fine furniture and silk-stocking accoutrements... Tiffany vases, gilded mirror frames, bone china and solid gold utensils.

But I couldn't fully enjoy the panoply set before me. Adrian, I had just found out, sat in jail some distance away, and only Dr. Bainbridge held the key to his freedom.

Elizabeth and I ate quietly. Soon, my muscles relaxed and my racing mind calmed. Sitting by the fire, which should have been intimidating, instead produced the opposite effect. It helped me unwind. I heard the gentle chiming of the grandfather clock in the corner of the room. Its rhythmic counting slowed my heartbeat. I placed my plate and fork back on the table for fear of dropping them should I nod off.

I settled back in my chair and, just as I allowed the soft cushioning to take the full weight of my body, I heard a ruckus outside the door that made Elizabeth and me stand and face the hallway.

"Anna, is that you?" she asked.

CHAPTER 22

DR. BAINBRIDGE

Monday, 10:00am

I told the driver to wait for me. I had never been inside a police precinct before, but I entered The Northern with all the bearing of my status in life and demanded to speak to the senior officer.

"I'm Captain Denton. What can I do for you, sir?"

"Are you holding a prisoner by the name of Adrian Crosby?"

"Let me check. Ah... yes, sir. He's being held pending charges."

"I'm Doctor Barton Bainbridge, the person who is pressing those charges."

"I see. Step right this way, if you please, so we can get the paperwork started."

"Just a minute, Captain."

"Yes?"

"I'd like to see Mister Crosby before I proceed."

"As you wish, sir. Follow me."

We walked down dimly lit hallways that smelled both foul and antiseptic, and passed men and some women in handcuffs being kept in line by officers holding truncheons in menace. Depravity was the real captive here. I was glad to get away from it as Captain Denton led me into his office.

"I must apologize for the conditions here. We are quite overcrowded. Many of the prisoners being held downtown had to be moved here because of the fire."

"Hmmm," I said, not really caring about their troubles.

The captain excused himself and went in search of Adrian. He was gone an interminable amount of time.

I was about to forget the whole thing when Adrian entered the room. He looked at me without recognition at first. I must have been a sight. Stubble shadowed my face and my dirty hair hung low over my forehead like a disguise.

"Doctor Bainbridge?" Adrian asked.

I started pacing. Pushing my hair free of my eyes, I glanced at Adrian, all the while trying to control my contempt.

"Sit down," Captain Denton said to his prisoner.

"Yes, sir," Adrian replied. "Doctor Bainbridge, do you have any news of Anna?"

"Don't..."

I fell into the pattern of lashing out at Adrian, caught myself quickly, then remembered what Elizabeth had said.

She found so much more in Adrian.

"I'm sorry to report, I do not. Captain, I'd like to speak to this man in private, if you don't mind."

Without a word, the officer left the room but stood just outside. I could see his hovering shadow against the glass door.

"Mister Crosby, I've... I've changed my mind. I'm not going to press charges against you."

"Doctor Bainbridge, I'm..."

"Don't thank me. Don't say a word. I need you to help me find my daughter. Come with me. I have a carriage waiting."

I opened the office door so fast that Captain Denton almost fell down. He regained composure quickly and put his hand on his gun. I waved him off with one sweep of the hand.

"No need, no need. I'm not pressing charges after all. I want this man freed right away."

"Very well. Mister Crosby, you may go."

"This way," I commanded.

"Wait, sir, please. I need to pick up the wedding bands taken from me when I was brought here."

"Make quick work of it. I won't wait all day."

After signing his release papers, Adrian received his rings. He dropped them in his pocket as he joined me at the carriage. I eyed him angrily for reminding me of my daughter's collusion to marry behind my back. But I kept my silence.

Adrian had trouble climbing up on the barouche's narrow step, so I steadied him from behind.

"Thank you, sir."

I hadn't the manners to respond. Instead, I directed the driver to take us as close to Saratoga Street as possible. I wanted to go home and see if my prodigal daughter had returned with her remorseful head in her hands.

During our trip, I opened *The Herald* to avoid conversation with my daughter's suitor. I perused the headlines, only pretending to be engrossed in the stories. As if my eyes deceived me, I leaned in closer to the paper to discern the type under a fuzzy photograph of the fallen fire chief. I gleaned the name *Anna Bainbridge* credited beneath the picture. Under that read: *Copyright Washington Post.*

"The unmitigated gall! How dare she? I am utterly appalled!"

All of the ire I had tried to put aside for the sake of finding my daughter coursed through my veins anew, so obvious, Adrian could feel its heat.

"What is it, sir? Nothing bad has happened to Anna, has it?"

Without offering an answer, I rolled up the paper and slapped it on my knee. As the coach slowed near home, I threw money at the driver, jumped down, and raced up the street, tripping on debris. This time, I didn't help Adrian, who almost fell trying to keep pace.

Pushing through the door with an angry gait, I startled Elizabeth and a man I didn't know in the parlor. There was a look of terror on his face. Elizabeth stepped between him and me to intercept my wrath. I could barely recognize the timbre of my own voice as I shouted.

"Look at this! Look at this!"

CHAPTER 23

ANNA

Monday, 1:00pm

I had to stop; my lungs were choked with smoke and fear. I couldn't go another step even though that strange man might still be following me. What did he want? In that one, quick encounter, I observed him a reed of a man, fair-skinned, with a thin voice and hair as blond as a field of wheat. I had never made his acquaintance before. And yet, he identified himself as Adrian's friend. Did I really hear that, or was the noise of the fire playing tricks on me? Did he mean me harm?

All along, I had been acting under a false sense of security. Behind the camera, I had used the lens as a suit of armor. I felt protected, apart from the surrounding cataclysm. As long as I looked through the viewfinder, I was sheltered from adversity. I couldn't be burned or hit by falling debris or accosted by a stranger. I forgot that the camera recorded an inverted image.

"Well, well, the little lady I've been looking for."

Another man addressed me... a more ominous man. His glaring eyes took me in, head to toe. Short, pallid and stocky, he spoke with the rasp of a heavy smoker. Thick black stubble protruded from his face like hundreds of prison bars. He smelled of every sin he had ever committed. Just the sight of him signaled danger. I took a big step back. He followed.

"A lot of people been lookin' for you, missy. But I'm the lucky one, I guess. I'm the one who's gonna win the big prize."

"What do you mean? Who are you?"

"A pal of that boyfriend of yours. He told me all about you, how you planned to run away, and how angry your rich father's gonna be when he finds out and..."

"I don't believe you're Adrian's friend. You're lying."

"You don't believe me? Then, how do I know all this?"

"Did Adrian send you?"

"Of course."

"What's your name?"

"Wilson... Cameron Clyde Wilson. But everybody calls me Will. And yours is Anna. And everythin' I've said is true. So, why don't you come with me, missy? I'll take you to Adrian, or your father, which is what I really want. Don't worry; he won't be upset. I'm thinkin' he might be so happy to see his little girl that he'll slip me more than a few bucks for rescuin' you."

"How do you know that? I don't trust you. No... no, I'm not going with you."

Will grabbed my arm like the clench of the fire, and pulled me into an alley.

"Now you look here, little lady. I'm gonna make my fortune on you. I ain't got much patience or time, so come on."

I didn't know what to do. This horrible man had dragged me away from the fire, away from other people. I had no idea what he was really up to, or where he might take me.

As soon as you trust yourself, you will know how to live.

Papa had drummed that quote by Goethe in my head; now I understood what it meant. I had learned a lot about myself these last two days and had wrestled with doubts. But I discovered one thing beyond all else. I was resourceful. For the most part, my decisions and instincts had paid off. I followed the fire; gave Mencken my pictures for publishing; and found ways to eat, drink and rest. And I blazed my own trail through a fire that destroyed just about everything else in its path. What's more, I did it on my own. Yes, I trusted myself.

Now I needed to work my way out of this dilemma. I figured if money could buy freedom, there must be another way for Will to get his payoff. I pulled a roll of unexposed film from my pocket. What was one more lie?

"Mister Wilson. This is a roll of film that I shot of the fire. I planned to sell these pictures to *The Herald* and the *Washington Post*. They're worth a lot of money. Maybe newspapers in other cities would pay for them, too."

"So what?" he growled.

"Well, if I give you the film, you'll be able to make your money from the sale, and therefore, you can let me go."

"Whaddya take me for? I don't know nothin' about cameras. I ain't never even seen one before. How do I know any of them pictures will fetch a dollar? Besides, you're worth a whole lot more to me than what's inside that box."

I wasn't about to fall prey to this man. Or get caught between two fires again. Remaining as calm as possible, I waited until I could figure out a way to make a successful escape.

"Hurry up, wouldya? I ain't got all day. My pocket and my belly are both empty."

I complied, if only to buy some time. Together, we looked like two implausible companions, lumbering along for blocks, with Will's arm locked in mine, giving the impression that we comprised a couple. When I saw that we were heading north towards home, I relaxed a little, thinking Wilson really would follow through on his scheme. He would take me home, receive his reward for delivering me safely to my father and be on his way. Things didn't work out as planned. Every time Will spotted a police officer, he pulled me out of sight behind a barrel or barricade, and when the coast became clear, he forced a detour. Soon the two of us drifted off course and ended up on East Saratoga and Guilford, an area untouched by the blaze and away from home.

"Anna! Anna! Over here. Hurry!" a man called out.

So taken aback by this unexpected outburst, Will let go of my arm for a split second. No wonder he acted so skittish. I discovered later that he had a police record as long as my arm.

I seized the moment and ran towards the voice that had come from a small crowd of people gathered on the opposite corner.

"I need you to get a picture," the man said.

I recognized him as one of Mencken's staff. For the time being, I was safe. Turning around, I saw that Will had disappeared as fast as he had come into my life.

My body shook from the ordeal and before I could compose the shot, I had to compose myself. I took long, soothing breaths of fresh air and pinched the delicate skin on my hand, as had been my habit when trying to calm down.

"Is something the matter?" the newspaperman asked.

"No, no. I'm just a little winded from running across the street. It's been a long day."

I didn't want to push my plight on anyone connected to H.L. Mencken. It would have been unprofessional. After a minute, I felt ready to get back to work. Buoyed by my freedom, I settled into a routine of seeking information, without saying a word to the reporter about my brush with that awful Cameron Clyde Wilson.

"What's all the fuss about here?" I asked.

"Most of the telegraph poles in the city are gone. This is the only one left close to the fire. The police are using it to call for more help, and the newspapers are sending copy via Morse code to other cities for publication."

"Right here on the street?"

"It's the best we can do."

"Who are these people? Are they all waiting to send messages?"

"When the fire struck our building, *The Herald* wasn't the only business to lose contact with the world. The offices of *Western Union* and *The Associated Press* were located there, too. These people worked for one or the other and they brought their telegraph instruments to this pole, where they're connecting with the one copper wire left to get the word out."

"How did you know there was a telegraph pole here?"

"Haven't you ever eaten at the House of Welsh?"

"The house of what?"

"The House of Welsh, right here on the corner. All newspaper reporters eat here."

"They do? Why?"

"Well, for one thing, it's close to our offices. Or, I should say, *was* close. Did you know that *The Herald* was destroyed last night?"

Fighting sudden tears, I couldn't respond. Finally, I said, "Go on."

"This restaurant is also close to City Hall and the Courthouse. Every lawyer, politician, and police official eats here. Besides, they have the best Welsh rarebit in town."

The building consisted of three row houses combined into one restaurant made of red brick but painted charcoal grey. The side of the building on the corner looked like a giant chalkboard menu. White letters at the very top read:

EST **1900**

THE HOUSE OF WELSH

STEAKS CHOPS

SEAFOOD

To the left towered a giant drawing of a medicinal-looking whiskey bottle and next to it in big, bold print... "Welsh's Black Bottle." The letters L-U-N-C-H vertically lined the edge of the building from top to bottom.

I could just imagine reporters inside, mingling with judges and the chief of police and the mayor, important men who filled their bellies with rare meat and rye whisky, then filled their lungs with cigar smoke. This was where reporters made their connections; this was where they got their scoops. Intrigued, I stepped back and took a wide frame of the building. Then moved in closer for a picture of someone tapping out Morse code on the pole. The way these people managed to get their jobs done, despite the catastrophe, despite having minimal resources, inspired me to keep going.

As I wound the film to the next frame, I thought about my run-in with Wilson. Just days ago, an encounter with a man of baseborn character would have been shocking. Today, it most assuredly frightened me, but it seemed to be just another layer of life that I had to contend with if I wanted to be a photojournalist. Most surprising was how quickly I had adjusted to working in the grit and gristle of the city, so far removed, yet just blocks away from home and all its safety and sterility and stuffiness. I thought maybe I was cut out for this lifestyle after all.

My confidence grew with *The Herald's* need for my services. I left the security of the crowd at the restaurant and walked towards the harbor, all the while keeping an eye out for Will... and the man who had called me by my full name. I thought they might be working together. If so, I would have to stay ever alert; it would be two against one from now on.

The sun burned at its brightest, so blinding it seemed as if the sky itself were on fire. A great deal of smoke had been blown in the opposite direction, where the largest number of firefighters attacked the blaze that still fumed, taking out its temper on the edge of the harbor.

Along the Jones Falls, down by the point where President Street met the water's edge, a fire flared up for the second time at Francis Denmead's Malt House. Firefighters thought they had put out the flames earlier, only to see them rise from the dead. The same thing had happened, not once, but three times in a lumberyard on Savannah Pier. Flare-ups dotted Baltimore for hours. Firefighters were not amused by this cat-and-mouse game. These little fires took attention away from the main blaze. They were demanding and demoralizing.

Everyone worked hard to keep the fire from jumping the Jones Falls and threatening Little Italy, a crisscross of narrow streets with a large population of immigrants crammed into row houses seemingly as thin as pasta. If the blaze were to spread there, fire trucks and water tower vehicles would barely have room to maneuver. Unchecked, the inferno might race right through Jonestown, Little Italy, and up the harbor water line to Fells Point, Canton, maybe even Highland Town. There would be no telling how destructive the fire would turn then. The manpower needed to fight such a blaze would far exceed what could be supplied, even if they called in fire departments from five more states.

By now, Chief Horton had recovered enough to return to the front, where firefighters had been working for well past twenty-four hours. For almost that long, units from all over Maryland and neighboring states had fought valiantly with their brothers. Harrisburg firefighters pumped water for the fifteenth hour straight. Baltimore City Police remained on duty beyond their normal shifts. Despite the wind blowing against it, *The Cataract* sprayed water continuously towards the fire. The National Guard had erected encampments throughout downtown, where they catnapped and ate in pitched tents between patrols. Private citizens kept supplying the men with food and water. Everyone resisted exhaustion. None more than me.

There was a feeling in the air that the end of the fire would be near... if it could be confined to the western side of the Jones Falls, a stream that snaked through Baltimore.

I had been with the blaze from the beginning; I would see it to the end. Hard as it was to admit, in a way, I didn't want it to be over. Mencken had once said his job was "exhilarating." Now I understood what he meant. Digging for information, writing down witness statements, taking pictures of something historically important gave me the same thrill. This would be my life's work, I thought. This would be my stamp on the world. Photojournalism had become comfortable, as fitting as my lost gloves. Even so, I didn't know where I'd end up and what would happen once the fire was all said and done.

For now, I carried on. Doing something, anything, became preferable to standing still. I'd had my fill of stagnant living.

Strange as it might seem, the last building to catch fire was the American Ice Company on West Falls Avenue. The blaze burned so close to the Jones Falls, that firefighters pumped water straight from the tributary to the burning building. They threw every resource and all the manpower they had at the fire.

I recorded much of it on film and in writing, at ease with asking questions and taking quotes to form a whole story.

At that point, I braced myself for the big standoff, one final push. But there wasn't one. The end did not arrive abruptly. The fire wouldn't truly be over for days, even weeks, as long as the tiniest whiffs of smoke still rose from the ashes and embers, tucked under debris, which continued to flicker, poised to erupt.

All the same, by five o'clock, just as darkness fell on its second day, the Great Baltimore Fire of 1904, though still burning, was officially declared "under control."

Mysteriously, at the same time, the wind died down. And Baltimore's lights and lampposts turned back on. It was by sheer coincidence that the city's master electricians, who had worked during the fire to restore power, succeeded at that moment.

Relief spread throughout Baltimore like electrical current. Except to photojournalist, Anna Bainbridge. My life was anything but "under control."

I had no idea where I stood with Papa, Adrian, Elizabeth, or even H.L. Mencken and *The Herald*. Now that firefighters had the upper hand, where would I go? What would I do? My fledgling career had been watered down and the flame of excitement that drove me these last two days had been extinguished.

"Think you can get away from me so fast, little lady?"

I had let my guard down. While pondering my future, I hadn't paid attention to the present. I hadn't kept a watchful eye on my surroundings. Regardless, I wasn't about to be led away again.

I caught a second wind. Whipping around, I took two steps back, held still for a split second, and snapped a picture of Cameron Clyde Wilson. The truth of him stuck to the film, however faint, due to the dim light of the setting sun. Nonetheless, it would be evidence in bringing him to justice.

Will lurched towards the camera. I channeled his violence. Using the chunky heel of my shoe, I stomped on his foot, right at the ankle, and shoved him with all my might. He fell to the ground with a loud growl and bounced right back up as if he were made of rubber. He limped in pain, danced in circles.

I took off running towards my neighborhood. Mentally, I had to take it one block at a time, just as I had taken it one brick at a time in the breezeway. I had found my freedom once; I would find it again.

Within a minute, Will was right behind me. He grunted and cursed. I felt the anger of his rotten breath on my neck. Somewhere along the way, his hatred lost its power and a more omnipotent force took over. I was able to run faster than I ever imagined.

Gradually, Will's scent grew faint. He didn't have the stamina to keep up. I refused to slow down. Just as I thought I must be home free, a firm hand clamped down on my shoulder and stopped me dead in my tracks.

CHAPTER 24

ADRIAN

Monday, 1pm

"What is it, Doctor Bainbridge?" Elizabeth asked.

Without saying a word, Anna's father threw *The Herald* on the table, stormed into his study and slammed the door. Elizabeth picked up the pages that had scattered to the floor. Sam helped her and, together, we scanned the paper to see what could have riled Dr. Bainbridge.

"Well, what do you know," I said with a smile. "That's my Anna."

"What is it? Will someone please tell me?" Elizabeth demanded. She squinted as if she had lost her glasses.

I asked if I could spread the newspaper out on the entry hall table. Granted permission, I smoothed the wrinkled folds so we could all see a picture with Anna's name listed as the photographer, right there at the top of the front page.

"Isn't she something?" I said.

Sam and Elizabeth bent down over the table and took a good look. Both rose back up in unison and stared at me in surprise.

"Now I understand why Doctor Bainbridge was so angry," Elizabeth said. "What I don't understand, Mr. Crosby, is why you are not."

"How can I be? Look at what Anna's accomplished with that little Brownie box camera. And under such extreme circumstances."

"She left you at the altar. Aren't you upset about that?" Elizabeth said.

"Well, I have to say... yes, I am disappointed and still terribly worried for her. But photography is part of who Anna is. I know it better than anyone. I love that about her. She gets excited about taking a picture of a plain buttercup. This fire is so much more. It's a huge, historical event. I would have been surprised if she hadn't run off to shoot pictures of it. My real concern is... when did she take this photograph? And what has she been doing since?"

"I saw her, Adrian, not more than a couple of hours ago. That's what I came here to tell everyone," Sam said.

"You saw Anna? Where?"

"Down at The Basin, right in the middle of the fire. I called her name but she ran away. I guess she became frightened because she didn't know me."

"How did she seem to you?"

"A little tattered and dirty but obviously unharmed. Beyond doubt, she's no worse for wear. She had enough energy to get away from me pretty fast."

I laughed with such heartiness I almost fell down. Both Elizabeth and Sam reached out to steady me.

"Thanks, Sam. You found her, and that means the world to me. So does your friendship."

Sam bowed his head in humility. The poor fellow wasn't used to being singled out or praised. He'd been through a war with nature and shown his valor. I thought him as true a hero as any infantryman.

The door to the doctor's study flew open, revealing Anna's father, still as angry as when he went in.

"I don't understand Anna. She's inconsiderate, impetuous, unruly... she's embarrassed me one time too many..."

"...and I'll be happy to take her off your hands, Doctor Bainbridge."

"Don't trifle with me, Mister Crosby. After what she's done to you, I'd think you'd be relieved that the wedding never took place."

"Quite the contrary, Doctor."

Dr. Bainbridge stepped closer and eyed me warily.

"What do you mean? Why?"

"It's simple, sir. I love Anna for the person she is. She's not perfect; neither am I. Before I met her, I was happy but longing for a woman like Anna. With her, I'm so much better off. My life is fuller when she's around. She sees the world in ways no one else does. I guess it's because of that camera of hers and what she's learned through her photography. Haven't you ever noticed that?"

"No, I can't say that I have."

"That's too bad, Doctor Bainbridge. Because the Anna I know sees the world in all its bigness, and detail, and delicacy and coarseness. She captures everything. She captures... life!"

Dr. Bainbridge waved his hand as if swatting away a revolting odor.

"I wish she had never bought that camera. It's caused nothing but trouble."

"Not so, Doctor. Anna tried many times to use her camera in attempts to get closer to you. She often talked of asking you to go out with her, to help her with her pictures. According to her accounts, you rarely seemed willing."

"I had work to do."

"So did Anna. This was her work."

"She's a girl. A girl of high social standing, who stood to inherit great wealth. Why does she want to work? She could join the Women's Sewing Bee, or The Garden Club, or perform good deeds through the church, as her mother did. Indeed, one of my compeers told me he saw Anna entering the Women's Industrial Exchange just blocks from our home. I was mortified."

"Why, Doctor Bainbridge? I've been there myself with Anna. It's a wonderful place, a place for women who have no other outlet to sell their craft. It helps women earn a decent living and even offers them lodging, if they need it."

"And Anna among them? Outrageous! It's beneath her. That's not how a daughter of mine should behave."

"Doctor Bainbridge, Anna is not misbehaving at all. She's simply an individual, living life her way."

"I don't have time to spar with you, Mister Crosby. We are never going to see eye to eye."

"We are agreed on that then. Now, don't you think it would be to everyone's benefit if we put our differences aside and worked together, just this once, to find Anna and bring her home? She must be terribly hungry and tired."

"She knows where she lives. She could have come home anytime she wanted."

"Could she? Maybe she's afraid to come home. Afraid of you."

"I don't answer to you, Mister Crosby. And I won't allow you to insult me any further in my own home. Now, you listen to me. Anna is a stubborn girl. You will learn it soon enough. Take that as a warning before you enter into marriage with my daughter. With this little foray of hers, she has taken me away from my own work, which is far more important than hers. And you want me to welcome her home with open arms?"

"What about what she's been through these last two days? Have you not thought about that, for even one second? Sir, I'm not going to continue arguing with you either, when we could be out there searching for Anna. Come, Sam, we must go. Oh, by the way, in case you are interested, Sam saw Anna just a few hours ago, taking pictures of the fire."

"Still?" Dr. Bainbridge replied.

"What do you mean... still?" Adrian asked.

"Nothing, nothing at all. I... I'm not... I'm tired. I must have misheard you."

I stared at Anna's father watchfully. Then chose not to pursue the matter. Not right then, anyway.

Sam nodded his appreciation for the hospitality Elizabeth had offered. He didn't dare look at the doctor. Instead, he helped me make my way to the front door. Just before we left, I turned around with one final comment for Anna's father.

I stepped closer and stared right into those large, dark eyes that now expressed unmistakable guilt. "I guarantee one thing, sir. Anna and I will be married as soon as possible, with or without your blessing. You will be free of her, if you choose. It will be completely up to you. And this is my warning. If you deny your daughter, it will break her heart. Think about that, Doctor Bainbridge. You don't deserve her love."

I kept staring at the doctor, as Elizabeth held the door for us. She whispered, "You're a good man, Mister Crosby. Godspeed."

Beyond her, I caught a glimpse of Dr. Bainbridge heading towards his study. He picked up a bottle of sherry just inside the door. There was no doubt he was imbibing, not to get drunk, but to wash down the tannins of disappointment in his daughter.

CHAPTER 25

ANNA

Monday, 6:00pm

"Where do you think you're goin'? Gimme that camera," Will said.

I twisted and turned until I wrenched free. Without hesitation, I kicked the pointed toe of my right boot straight up under the bristly chin of Cameron Clyde Wilson. His head reared back like Goliath's had when he was scorched by the explosion at the Hurst building. In an effort to shake off the pain, Will stomped his foot, then hobbled in a circle just as that fire horse had done.

I didn't wait to see what Wilson would do next. I took off like a shot and ran directly to a National Guard tent posted nearby. No one stood watch there. I darted back out, searching for a soldier. I found one, probably younger than I, patrolling a half block away.

"Please, please help me," I cried.

I reached the guardsman's side and looked back, only to see Will meld with the detritus. As we walked to the tent, I blurted my story. The soldier directed me to wait inside, and help myself to coffee, an apple and a blanket. He gave Wilson's description to members of his division, who went in search of him.

"Thank you for the refreshments."

"You're welcome, ma'am. It would be best if you stayed out of sight until we capture the villain."

"I promise you, I won't leave your watchful eye. I'm just too tired."

"I have to continue my patrol down the block. You'll be safe here alone. Sit back and relax. You look like you've been through the mill, if you don't mind me saying so, ma'am."

As I stared at the soldier's back growing smaller and distant, something white skittered towards me. It landed at my feet like a missive from God. But it was only an envelope addressed to a man in New York. The seal was broken and the corner of a letter, peeking out, begged to be read. I picked it up and stepped inside the tent, where I was protected from the wind, the invisible kidnapper that still wanted its payoff.

Here, I eased into the kind of calm and quiet I hadn't felt since sleeping in church the day before, when I read another letter, one meant for my eyes only.

I sat down on the cot to gain my bearings and adjust my eyes. As soon as I lifted my sore feet off the ground, I realized how swollen they were. The soles burned cold and felt too big for my shoes. And my back ached. I felt a nest of knots in my hair, filled with bits of charred wood. When I looked down at my dress and jacket, metallic flecks and particles of dirt and tiny beads of glass imbedded in the fibers glistened as if they'd been woven there. I had to laugh.

"What a mess I've made of myself. No wonder that soldier said I looked like I'd been through the mill."

The letter that had floated into my possession contained all the mystery of Elizabeth's. It seemed to warm my hands. A burning curiosity pushed reason and propriety aside. In an effort to justify my nosiness, I vowed to send it off to its rightful recipient once I had extracted its words and inhaled its story.

It had been written within the hour, and somehow, after being posted, broke free. Perhaps, sent in haste.

February 8th, 1904
Dear Father:

It is 5pm in Baltimore. There is grave danger here and I am frightened. A fire. I know I told you I would be careful when I moved to the big city to become a dentist. However, sometimes there are circumstances beyond one's control.

It's difficult to reconcile why this might have happened. Wasn't it a cow tipping over a lantern that started the Great Chicago Fire just a few decades ago? Could it be that simple here?

After more than a day of blowing this way and that, like the zigging and zagging of a hungry grey squirrel, the blaze has burned through most of downtown. I fled to safety at a friend's place, where I write this horror story.

Looking out of his kitchen window towards the east, I see flames creeping up the side of the building that houses my practice. The fire seems to be everywhere. When will this hell end? Pardon my impolite language, Father. I am unstrung. All of Baltimore suffers.

There are firefighters, police and the National Guard trying to end this tragedy. Yet the fire continues. I heard stories of looters and cutpurses roaming the streets, stealing amidst vulnerability.

You probably want me to come home. I am not asking for that or any assistance. I will see this through and hope my office and records and instruments are salvageable. I ask only for your prayers.

Your devoted son,
Michael

The last few lines I read through a scrim of tears. Such tenderness between son and father. I was envious of their relationship even though just moments ago they had been strangers to me.

I put the letter back in its envelope, more resolved to see it delivered to its rightful owner. I felt ashamed to have interloped upon something so personal. But now I better understood the value of Adrian's work in connecting people, allaying fears, sharing lives. He was no *prole*. His profession was just as important as my father's.

"Papa," I said, missing him.

Inside this tiny tent, I felt more alone than ever. I had no place to go except inward. It pained me. I knew I had been lost to Papa and Adrian, separated by a world of self-discovery traveled in the short span of two days.

Even though my relationship with Papa had been strained and often one-sided, I loved my father, if for nothing else but that I recognized our similarities. We were both independent, direct, terse. But there were differences too, that had been starting to separate us. And the wedge was my fiancé.

Around Adrian, I cut a more approachable figure. My hard edges smoothed. My straightforwardness curved politely. I opened to new things. As a couple, we had come to enjoy popular music and two-stepping in public dance halls; riding bicycles in the park; taking rowboats out on the lake, and eating shaved ice flavored with egg custard, a Baltimore tradition; and laughing and cuddling. Adrian had been patient in teaching me how to ride a bicycle-built-for-two, and how to dance to the three-quarter meter of a slow waltz. In no time, we had graduated to the jazz waltz. I wasn't blessed with grace, but in Adrian's arms, I felt light and happy-go-lucky. What I lacked in poise, I made up for in tireless enthusiasm.

I thought about all that Adrian had given me. A blush of regret bloomed on my cheeks. "Adrian," I sighed, missing him even more than Papa.

I thought back to the previous morning when I stood with Monsignor Vilkas in church, so close to saying my wedding vows. Everything had been planned and timed to the minute. And none of it had happened, not only because of the fire. Mostly, because of me. My broken promise to marry Adrian pressed against my moral backbone like a swan-bill corset.

I hadn't even taken the time to jot a quick note, explaining my actions, for Monsignor Vilkas to hand him. And here, this stranger had written a well-thought-out letter to his father. What was wrong with me?

I wondered why I had really run away from the church. Was it merely because of the fire and my desire to document it on film? Or was I running to my work the way Papa ran to his? To avoid relationships. To avoid real emotional commitment. Was it second nature for me to adopt my father's willingness to escape at every opportunity? Papa to the immediacy of life and death... me to the immediacy of danger and destruction.

It dawned on me that all my life I had viewed my father and our relationship in individual frames, never seeing the bigger picture... until now.

I understood Papa better because I understood myself. My heart went out to him. Despite the bitter cold outside, the warmth of this revelation blanketed me. I wanted nothing more than to reconcile with Papa, that is, if he was willing.

And what about Adrian? Had he been just a means to this end? Had he been a substitute father? Had he taken me places and spent dedicated time with me that I had longed to share with Papa? Maybe, in the beginning, but no more. Our love was real. I felt sure of it. Knowing what I knew then, if Adrian and Monsignor Vilkas were to walk into the tent at that moment, would I still have gone through with the wedding?

That question I couldn't answer. It was too definitive. Too final. So much had happened in the last couple of days. Was I the same person Adrian fell in love with? Would he still want me?

Then, there was H.L. Mencken. As repugnant as his nature was, he had taken me under his wing and taught me how to become a photojournalist. And he did it during a time when he had been under tremendous pressure to write, edit and publish a newspaper. He had trusted my work and taken my film for publishing. I would be forever indebted for his generosity. I wished I could thank him. If he were to come into the tent and offer me a job at *The Herald*, would I have taken it? Would I take it without conferring with Adrian or Papa? Once again, no answer.

I didn't think the inability to decide my future then and there showed immaturity. Quite the opposite. I was finally giving these questions the weight of thought they deserved.

Despite all the uncertainty, I had renewed hope in the future, whatever it might bring. At least, I knew I would never go back to being alone and aimless, the rich doctor's daughter with nothing to do. No matter what came next, it would be exciting. I promised myself.

I stood and stretched my tight muscles. I looked down at the cot and realized that, for the past hour, I had not touched my camera once. It sat idle, unattached to me, cold from lack of light. I picked it up, unwilling to retire my Brownie another minute, even though it was dark outside and there was diminished firelight to shoot by.

I stepped out of the tent, leaving my past behind for the second time. I faced the future, as boundless as the outdoors.

Drawing in a deep breath, I thought I smelled the last man on earth I would ever miss. But he was nowhere in sight.

Chapter 26

DR. BAINBRIDGE

Monday, 6:00pm

Enough of Anna and her self-interests. It was time to return to the security of my work at the hospital. I was needed there. I really wanted to go so I could feel like myself again. And after the dressing down I had endured at Adrian's hands, I was too embarrassed to stay home. Because of what had transpired earlier, I couldn't look Elizabeth in the eye. She probably sided with Adrian and I wasn't about to let my own servant chide me further, not even with a look.

I shouldn't have been drinking before work. It was truly most odd. But I raised the bottle to my lips anyway, then paused. Just shy of taking a sip, I wondered if I really had been a poor father. Hadn't I provided for Anna? Given her everything? She lived in a home grander than most, with a featherbed, warming fires, and plenty to eat. I had seen to her education and religious instruction in accordance with Victoria's wishes. Anna was sheltered from experiencing any of life's difficulties and tragedies, including how her mother had suffered and died. In her stead, I had put Elizabeth, a well-educated woman, in charge of Anna's daily care while I earned the living that gave my daughter all that a young girl needed. What more could she have possibly wanted? What did she find in Adrian that was lacking in the life I had given her?

It wasn't that I disliked Adrian. In fact, I had grown to respect him these last two days. He had presented himself as a man of his word; he seemed honorable and obviously a gentleman, although of poor social standing and meager income. I always wanted a man of means and status for my daughter. But her stubborn independence put an end to my plans time and time again. She projected too much self-importance to stand in someone else's shadow. So I gave up. I figured Anna could take care of herself as a single, wealthy woman. Yet, I couldn't understand why she refused my attempts to tame her wild ambitions. Didn't she trust my ability to know better? Why was she fixated on photography? Why was she interested in pursuing a man's occupation? The embarrassment Anna brought me made me wince.

Planning to return to the hospital as soon as I was presentable, I thought I would wash and shave. I put down the bottle and noticed a book on my desk. It was called *Medicine and the Empathetic Heart*. This had been a gift from Victoria a few years into my career. I had occasionally administered to prisoners brought to the hospital from the Maryland State Penitentiary not far away. Victoria had heard me complain often of having to care for these hardened criminals, when so many deserving people had to wait for medical treatment. She thought my resentment unfounded. People in need were equals, regardless of their actions.

The book was written by a doctor and a minister, who saw the deplorable conditions in prisons in the early 1850s and fought for compassionate care for all people, even the most debased and cruel.

I guess Victoria's gift was meant to make me more considerate, more understanding. I wouldn't know; I had never read the book. And she never asked my opinion of it.

Why was it sitting dead center on my desk? Had Elizabeth dusted it and then forgotten to return it to the shelf?

Splitting pages 6 and 7 was a deep red velvet bookmark. I certainly had not placed it there.

Opening the book, I lifted the divider and felt as if separating the past and future. I shivered from a cold sensation not unlike a wind gust, unexplained in the stuffy, closed-off atmosphere of my office. I began to read.

Treating patients solely based on education and intelligence proves a disservice to patient

and doctor. The medical provider must feel what the patient feels.

I had always prided myself on my capacity for knowledge and high intelligence. Yet, I admit to feelings of superiority. For a moment, I explored their incompatibility. Then, my eyes continued to peruse the page.

Medical staff must open themselves to the patient's total experience... pain, disease, and emotional and psychological effects on the body and mind. The only way to do this is to feel. The only way to treat the patient is with kindness.

"Kindness," I murmured. *"Kindness."* I was a great doctor and teacher. I knew that. I fixed hearts plagued by disease. I saw patients expecting to die, instead return to their families and jobs. I made the impossible happen. Uplifting a sagging spirit, or calming fears of suffering and death and what followed had never seemed important.

I never thought compassion fit on the apothecary shelf. The closer a physician came to feeling a patient's pain, the more pain was placed between his own shoulder blades, the weight that of Atlas. Always better to keep a safe distance.

A safe distance. Anna's image appeared in my mind like a cathode ray inside a vacuum tube. It suddenly occurred to me that I had built a glass enclosure around her, disregarding her unique light inside. I treated her as a patient, not a daughter. Perhaps I had even done the same with Victoria. Maybe that's why she gave me the book in the first place.

I snapped the covers shut and shuddered once again as a waft of cold air lifted from the pages and chilled my soul. I couldn't catch my breath and became soaked to the skin with sweat, the afterbirth of a man just given a second chance at life. Tears rolled down my face. I sensed Victoria so near. I searched all around the room for my wife but she was nowhere. I spoke to her out loud as if she could hear me.

"I'm so sorry, Victoria. I wasn't the husband I promised you I would be. I haven't been a proper father to Anna. What should I do?" No one answered.

With confession comes restitution. I needed to make amends. For Anna's sake, and in order to bring peace to my own life, I had to reconcile with her and allow her to be herself, make her own choices in life. It's what Victoria wanted of me.

I self-imposed the penance... to face my own shame. I had to take the blame for not being there for Anna most of her life, just as I hadn't been there for my wife that one fateful, tragic week.

At that time, so young and gifted, I had just received a promotion at the hospital. It went to my head like fine sherry. I celebrated my own importance and the congratulations of the Board of Directors and my new staff. There were plenty of presentations to prepare, new students to acclimate, an influx of patients to treat, and submissions to medical journals to write. My work would bring a higher level of prestige to the hospital and to me. For that one week, I wasn't home much. I wasn't there to notice my wife scratching the bright red lines marking the folds of her elbow. I wasn't there to see the rash staining her porcelain neck, or the texture of her skin turn to sandpaper, her tongue to strawberry red. I wasn't there to perceive a white ring circle her mouth. I wasn't there to feel her forehead for the heat of fever. And neither was Elizabeth, who sat bedside with her own ailing mother elsewhere.

It had been unlike Victoria to complain. She would never have taken me away from my work, not at a pivotal point in my career. Before we both knew it, it was too late. Thankfully, while Elizabeth was away, Anna had been put under the care of the nuns at the church convent, where she was spared.

But why couldn't I have saved Victoria? How could I have made this one, fatal, irreversible error?

Over my long career, I had seen many people pass. I always felt bad when they were my own patients. But I knew, better than anyone, that sometimes even the best medical care isn't enough. People die. It was inevitable. That's what I kept telling myself to keep emotion from creeping into my work, from penetrating the vacuum. Now I realized that each of those patients had been a "Victoria" to someone.

A new feeling washed over me. One I had never felt, at least not for a long time. It seemed so new, so warming. What was it? Possibly, compassion?

Deep down, it felt good. It exuded the kind of love that erased all memory of transgressions and all foretelling of future mistakes, no matter how egregious.

I realized my daughter needed her father's unconditional love. *My* unconditional love.

I understood that many of Anna's actions corresponded to the way I had treated her. Yes, she was churlish and willful. But I was complicit in how she had turned out. I hoped it wasn't too late to breathe new life into our relationship. I longed for that second chance that resuscitation provided.

"Thank you, Victoria," I said out loud.

I couldn't sit and wait for Adrian and Sam to find my daughter and bring her back home. I wanted to show Anna how much I cared about her. I needed to be the one to find her, no matter how awful the surroundings, no matter how embarrassing it might be for me to be seen under such vile circumstances by someone from the hospital or the Board of Directors. As uncomfortable as I felt and as disheveled as I looked, I left my study, grabbed my coat and ran out the door before Elizabeth could utter a word or stare me in the eye.

CHAPTER 27

ANNA

Monday, 9:00pm

After walking around a while, I got lost in the crowd of onlookers and was pushed back to the corner of Eutaw and Fayette. For the longest time, police and National Guardsmen kept us behind barricades until firefighters said we could safely wander around The Basin.

I headed east as far as I could go and ended up just north of the Power Plant, which remained one of the few buildings still standing, even though it stood so close to the place where the blaze had made its final surge. I thought I could squeeze one final story and photograph out of the fire.

All around, firefighters watered down rubble and loaded unused equipment back on their trucks. Units from other cities that were no longer needed packed up in preparation for their return home. Private citizens owning large wagons continued to earn money by hauling away debris that showed no signs of catching fire again. Police and National Guardsmen stood by to keep order. Spectators lined Little Italy's side of the Jones Falls and government officials crept closer to assess loses.

Despite the activity, I was alone in the burned-out mess. Just thinking about reuniting with my family filled me with the energy to go on, despite heartache and fatigue. A desperate need to be with Adrian consumed me. But another man, bent on seeking revenge, made it to my side first.

"Hello, little lady."

Will wrapped a tight fist around my left wrist. This time there was no wrangling and letting go. He yanked my arm hard and I yelled for help. No one responded.

So I used the only weapon I had that might grant freedom, the same weapon I had used for liberation from my previous life. My camera.

With my right hand firmly wrapped around the strap of my Brownie, I whacked my captor across the temple. I watched in horror, not at the damage inflicted on Wilson. Instead, at the tiny pieces of my camera as they dropped to the ground. All that remained was the top lid of the Brownie and the strap, still attached to my hand. Will lost his grip.

"You're a vexing, evil, horrible man. Look at my camera. Look what happened to it," I said.

With that, I screamed with all the might of my five-foot frame. I kicked Wilson and bashed him nonstop. He wasn't badly hurt by any of the blows, but so stunned by my boldness, he couldn't move. He just stood there and took it. I increased the intensity of my thrashing.

Then, Will felt something cold and steely clamp down on his own wrist. A police officer had slapped a handcuff on Cameron Clyde Wilson, ending his freedom once and for all.

"We've been looking for you, Wilson."

"Yeah, so what?" Will growled.

"Miss, are you all right?"

"I'm fine. But my camera didn't fare so well."

"That can be replaced. You'll have to come to the precinct to make a statement, so we can press charges. Did he try to steal your camera? If so, it'll be one more offense we'll add to a long list."

"Can we talk about this tomorrow? I really want to go home right now."

"Certainly, miss. We're taking him back to The Northern. He gave us the slip there last night. We've been searching for him ever since. Believe me, he won't be getting out again any time soon."

"That makes me feel better. Thank you."

I looked down at what remained of my camera. The film on the roll that had been inside it had unspooled and now lay exposed. It seemed that my faults... rudeness and capriciousness and my stubborn streak... had been exposed, too.

Maybe it was good that these flaws had come to light. Maybe it would be better not to replace them.

I left the mess where it had fallen. It would be buried with all the other casualties of the fire... the buildings, the businesses, the banks. It seemed only fitting. These were pieces of me that would remain relics of the fire, particles of bone found in the pyre, proof that a sacrifice had been made here.

Relieved but weary, I left the encampment and walked out into the night. Standing on the southwestern corner of Pratt and President Streets, I searched for the safest route to take, for once.

Darkness and a dense cloud of smoke hung low over Baltimore, a gaunt reminder of the tragedy that had befallen the city these last two days. Through the misty shroud, I spotted a tall man coming towards me from the northern corner of the intersection. At first, I thought he might be that mysterious reed of a man who had called out to me hours earlier. I backed away in apprehension. Like a specter, he moved slowly out of the shadows. The haze melted away, and he stepped into a silvery beam of moonlight that illuminated one side of his face. He looked like a forlorn version of my father, no better off than Wilson. He seemed debased, unclean, not at all the picture of decorum my father always represented. I couldn't believe my eyes.

"Papa?" I called out.

"Anna," he said tenderly.

I wanted to run to him but remained hesitant. I needn't have worried; Papa rushed to me. He took me in his arms, his body as tall and strong as a maple. His embrace felt warm and genuine and unrestrained. I reciprocated with all my heart.

I had dreamed of this moment as long as I could remember. Father and daughter, holding each other so tightly even gale force winds couldn't have parted us.

"Papa," was all I could utter.

"My Anna," he said, as he kissed the top of my head over and over again.

I fought back tears but couldn't. Neither one controlled the emotions that flowed like the Jones Falls. Both of us surrendered to the current of the moment.

The blaze had not destroyed our family after all. Rather, its intense heat had made us malleable. Our hearts had become annealed, forged in a new resolve... to build our relationship into what it should have been all along.

As I rested my head close to Papa's heart, I didn't think life could get any better. Until I heard the sweet, familiar lyrics of a popular parlor song.

"*In the good ole summertime...*"

I moved back just a half step, unwilling to let go of my father completely. Looking around his shoulder, I saw Adrian, leaning on a crutch, singing what had become our own private paean. I raced to his arms.

Dear Sam, that blessed reed of a man, such a gallant soul, didn't wait for his rightful due. He backed away, made his exit and faded into the confusion that protected this intimate family reunion.

"Anna, you're safe. I'm so happy," Adrian whispered.

I took a good look at my fiancé.

"But, what happened to you, Adrian? Did you get hurt because of me?"

"I would have risked anything, even death, trying to find you."

A clot of guilt in my throat blocked words of regret from reaching my lips. I couldn't believe that Adrian and Papa hadn't admonished me, or worse, rejected me. How could I have been this lucky?

"Papa... Adrian..."

"No talking now," my father said. "There will be plenty of time for that. I know you want to tell us everything. And I have something to say to you. Anna, I will answer the questions you have about your mother, all of them. It's time you knew the truth. Right now, we should take you home. You need food and rest."

I looked from one man to the other.

"Where is my home?" I asked.

I couldn't believe the metamorphosis that had taken place in me over these last two days. I was even more surprised at the transformation in Papa. What had brought him to this place? Why the change of heart?

And Adrian. Ardent as ever, still dependable. After all I had made him endure.

Just as the stars and stripes had waved proudly over Fort McHenry when the smoke of warring guns cleared, Adrian had been my banner, still there when the smoke of the Great Baltimore Fire of 1904 dissipated. Throughout his own battle with the fire, Adrian had kept his heart open to accept me as I was. How could I not want to be with him? Papa pulled me into his embrace once more. My loneliness blew away like the last puffs of smoke from the fire. My life had not crumbled in ruins. I would get a new beginning and so would the city I loved.

All the while, the fingers of my right hand still wound around the strap attached to the remnants of my Brownie. With all the shedding of skin, and with all the swirling of doubts, I knew one thing hard-and-fast. I would replace my Brownie. And when I did, I would slip my fingers around the handle and feel the power at hand once more. And, no matter what else happened from that day forward, I would never, ever, let go.

In heavenly confluence, a wisp of wind brushed my hair and kissed me on the cheek. I could have sworn that all the searing smells of the city had somehow dissipated, and the nuance of rosewater had filled the air.

AUTHOR'S NOTES

The Great Baltimore Fire of 1904 was an actual event, considered one of the worst fires in U.S. history. Its cause rests on speculation to this day. But the damage is clear. Destroyed were 86 blocks and 1500 buildings spread over 140 acres. Most were businesses, displacing 35,000 workers. As for the cost, the fire totaled approximately $130 million in 1904 monetary value.

I've tried my best to stay true to what happened over those two fateful days and to accurately portray the social mores of the era. I altered the time line on some events slightly for the sake of the narrative.

The story of Anna and Adrian is fictitious and so are their names. However, their characters were written in tribute to two of my relatives, one devoted to the fire's history and the other to Kodak Brownie cameras.

The Great Baltimore Fire of 1904 came alive to me through the firsthand accounts of my great uncle, Adrian Bell. I never tired of his stories. He lived a simple, fun-loving life. A postman by vocation and historian by avocation, he kept all the newspapers published immediately after the fire and shared them with family, friends and college students until his death at age 94. My love for Brownie cameras stems from the many times I smiled into one as my aunt, Anita Williams, smiled back while snapping the picture. She documented my family's gatherings through several decades. I am proud to own her Brownie Target Six-20.

The depiction of H.L. Mencken, though a legendary newspaperman, is also fictitious, but I based his personality on descriptions provided me by people who knew him and books written about him, including his autobiography, *Newspaper Days* (Knopf, 1941). He could often be found with a cigar in his hand because his father had owned a smoke shop and encouraged his son to join the family business when he became a man. Mencken acquiesced in silent protest, putting his dream of becoming a journalist on hold until his father's death.

The *Washington Post* did help *The Baltimore Herald* publish its fire edition and other D.C. papers offered their services to the remaining local publications. All of Baltimore's newspaper buildings were burned out and their owners had to scramble to find other means to keep going.

Ironically, photographs, etchings and engravings from the fire and the era proved to be my best resources. I found pictures of Mullin's Hotel, The Carrollton and its menu, *The Herald's* building, House of Welsh, O'Neill's, various churches and several other locations mentioned in the story. I also secured pictures of firefighters, police, detectives, the National Guard and fire spectators. Thanks to these photos, I was able to provide a great deal of detail.

I am especially grateful to Michael at the Enoch Pratt Free Library, Maryland's State Library Resource Center, for allowing me to use the cover photograph of firefighters spraying water on a building at German and Liberty Streets. The cover is also enhanced by the image of a young woman resembling the fictional Anna. It was taken from the "Holidays are Kodak Days" advertisement. Thank you, Joshua, from the Ellis Collection of Kodakiana, David M. Rubenstein Rare Book and Manuscript Library, Duke University, for granting permission to use it. Also, many thanks to Bonnie, from the Johns Hopkins Sheridan Libraries, for the map of Baltimore.

I am indebted to the firefighters and historians who keep the fire's story alive at the Fire Museum of Maryland, located in Lutherville, Baltimore County. Actual fire apparatus used to battle the 1904 blaze are on display there, including a water tower and an alarm system employed to rally units from all over the area. The museum's films of the fire and horses in action put me in Anna's shoes.

An enlarged photo portrait of Fire Chief Horton can be found at the museum. He made a full recovery from his injuries and so did fire horse, Goliath. Considered a hero by Baltimoreans, the horse found celebrity in leading parades and making appearances at various community events until his natural death in 1913. He was given a lengthy obituary in the *Baltimore Sun*, longer than any human being's write-up that day.

Mayor McLane did not fare so well. Following the fire, this hopeful statement, made by the mayor, appeared in *The Baltimore News*:

"To suppose that the spirit of our people will not rise to the occasion is to suppose that our people are not genuine Americans. Chicago dates her greatness from the great fire of 1871; Boston's fire in 1872... stimulated Boston's improvement and development; even little Galveston, overwhelmed by a flood which seemed calculated to wipe out all hope and courage in that town, rose up after the calamity more vigorous and more aggressive than ever. Baltimore will do likewise. We shall make the fire of 1904 a landmark not of decline, but of progress."

The mayor would not live to see these promises come to fruition. Just three months after the fire, he was found dead, a spent gun by his body.

He was not the only casualty. Reports vary but, suffice it to say, at least a few people died during the fire. One newspaper reported that the body of a badly burned African American male was found in the harbor waters. In addition, some emergency workers, who suffered singed palates and lungs, contracted pneumonia and succumbed within days of the fire. Among them, Fireman James Montgomery McGlennen, who fought the blaze from the first alarm on the morning of February 7th and worked the fire and its aftermath until Wednesday, February 10.

It was reported in an Irish newspaper that Martin Mullin, proprietor of Mullin's Hotel, died from fire injuries in March, 1904. Sol Ginsburg survived unharmed, but his business burned to the ground. I could find no evidence that he rebuilt.

At the time of the fire, The Alexander Brown & Sons building was only three years old. Though within the hot spot of the fire, it survived because of its size, only two-stories, dwarfed by skyscrapers in the same block. When the fire neared the building, a sudden updraft of wind leap-frogged the fire over Alex Brown to the next building. The stone façade suffered only a minor crack, never patched, and still visible. More importantly, the building's main feature, a dome-shaped stained glass skylight, designed by Gustave Baumstark, who studied under Louis C. Tiffany, withstood the heat and flames and can be enjoyed by visitors today.

Another surviving building, the Mercantile Trust & Deposit Co., dating to 1888, boasted in its post-fire advertising: "The contents of our vaults were unharmed by the Baltimore Fire of 1904." Recently refurbished inside to replicate the Globe Theatre, it now serves as the home of the Chesapeake Shakespeare Company. The original vault was incorporated into the design.

McCormick Spice and The Maryland Institute College of Art rebuilt elsewhere and thrive today.

The Church of the Messiah was also resurrected with the help of money raised by creating 2,800 small souvenir bells cast from its steeple church bell, which cracked irreparably during the fire. The current congregation now worships at their location on the corner of Harford Road and White Avenue in Hamilton.

There were many positive outcomes of the fire. National firefighting standards were upgraded. Units in each state were advised to either conform to standardized hydrant couplings or, at least, create adaptors. Guidelines for setting up command centers in catastrophes were refined. And, while rebuilding, engineers included a modern sewage system, which became a model for other cities.

Baltimoreans will find information in this book that appears inconsistent with modern times. So, I will set the record straight here and now. McLane Place was renamed Park Avenue. German Street became Redwood. Where City Hospital stood at the time now stands Mercy Medical Center. The Baltimore harbor's nickname evolved from The Basin to the Inner Harbor. And piers that used to have names like Dugan and Savannah now go by pier numbers. In 1904, the area north of Little Italy, flanked by the Jones Falls and Central Avenue, was called Jonestown. The House of Welsh existed at its Guilford Avenue location until

1998, when it moved to Fenwick Island, Delaware, and later closed. The Gothic building that housed the Northern District Police was repurposed as office space called "The Castle." Northern district operations moved to a modern facility nearby. The Power Plant retains its name but not its function. It's become an entertainment hub in downtown Baltimore with a giant Hard Rock Café guitar decorating its exterior. The Main Post Office moved to new quarters east of downtown, while the Italian building became a Baltimore City courthouse.

At the time of the fire, Patterson Park did have a lake, freely enjoyed by city residents. Though the park now boasts many attractions, such as the Victorian pagoda, the lake no longer exists.

The *Baltimore Herald* folded two years after the fire, leaving H.L. Mencken without a job. He was soon hired by *The Baltimore Sun*, where he stayed until a stroke forced his retirement. St. Alphonsus Church remains a gathering place for Catholic worshippers but its school no longer exists. Electric Park entertained Baltimoreans from 1896 to 1915 on 24 acres near the intersection of Belvedere Avenue and Reisterstown Road.

O'Neill's Department Store served elite customers until 1954, when management lost the lease on the building. A devout Catholic, Thomas O'Neill died, ironically, on Passion Sunday in 1919. Among donations elsewhere, he bequeathed an enormous amount of money to the Catholic Church, as he had promised God in exchange for sparing his business. The money was used to build the Cathedral of Mary Our Queen on North Charles Street in Baltimore, where O'Neill's stained glass image can be found in the chapel.

Though a longtime dream of mine to tell this story, the novel never would have taken shape without the help and support of Demi Stevens. More than an editor and guide through the process of publishing, she is an author's best friend, always focused on the positive. I can't wait to work with her again. I am also indebted to the teachers and students at Renaissance Institute at Notre Dame of Maryland University. Their nonjudgmental criticism proved invaluable in elevating my skills and my spirit throughout the development of my first novel.

I must also thank my sister-in-law, Karolyn Bertling for raising the bar. And my friend, Karen Williams, for never mincing words.

I am particularly grateful for a forty-year broadcasting career, mostly at WJZ-TV in Baltimore, one of the finest television stations in the country. It was there that I learned the value of commitment, relentless focus on reporting accuracy, and an unmatched standard of writing.

I used several historical resources in writing this novel:

BOOKS:

The Great Baltimore Fire – Peter B. Peterson

Baltimore Afire – Harold A. Williams

Forged By Fire – Maryland's National Guard At The Great Baltimore Fire of 1904 – Dean K. Yates

Goliath: Hero Of The Great Baltimore Fire – Claudia Fridell

Baltimore's Historic Parks And Gardens – Eden Unger Bowditch

Kodak Cameras, The First 100 Years – Brian Coe

Cameras From Daguerreotypes To Instant Pictures – Brian Coe

Collector's Guide To Kodak Cameras – Joan McKeown and James McKeown

The Skeptic: A Life Of H.L. Mencken – Terry Teachout

Thirty-Five Years Of Newspaper Work: A Memoir – H.L. Mencken (Henry Louis)

Newspaper Days – H.L. Mencken

MUSEUMS & HISTORICAL SOCIETIES:

Fire Museum of Maryland – 1301 York Road, Lutherville, Maryland 21093

Society For Historical Archaeology

Maryland Historical Society

NEWSPAPERS & MAGAZINES:

The Baltimore Sun

The Daily Record

The New York Journal

Style Magazine

Article entitled "Hot Numbers" by Miss Anna Schmidt

LIBRARIES:

Photographs and newspaper articles from 1904 and other written resources found at Enoch Pratt Free Library and Baltimore County Public Library.

I also found many helpful websites:

WEBSITES:

welcometobaltimore.com

baltimorefire1904.blogspot.com

pattersonpark.com

kilduffs.com

history.com

brownie-camera.com

kodak.com

americaninventors.blogspot.com

doloresmonet.hubpages.com

I hope you enjoyed reading this book and will forever remember the Great Baltimore Fire of 1904 as a benchmark for rebuilding what locals now affectionately call Charm City.

Book Club Questions

How does the title represent the story?

Did you feel sympathy for Anna's father?

How did danger trigger change in the characters?

In your mind, does Anna choose to marry Adrian?

Must we always marry within our own social strata?

Was Anna really in love with Adrian or was he a substitute father?

Anna's mother guides her through the wind. Did you enjoy this touch of magical realism?

Must women suffer to attain their dreams?

Is Anna justified in lying, stealing, and cursing under duress?

Was Anna selfish in her choices?

How has the novel made you examine your own relationships?

What does the chatelaine symbolize?

ABOUT THE AUTHOR

Donna Bertling holds a BA in English Literature from Loyola College (now Loyola University Maryland). She loves to inform and entertain through historical fiction, her favorite genre to read. Donna runs the Open Studio for Prose Writers at Renaissance Institute, Notre Dame of Maryland University. Several of her short stories have been published in *Reflections*, the institute's literary and art publication.

Author Photo by Norbert Bertling, Jr.

51967134R00116

Made in the USA
Middletown, DE
15 November 2017